The

Architect

and his

Muse

Susan M Higgins

An Amazon paperback

First published in December 2022

ISBN number 9798834295853

Disclaimer

The Architect and his Muse is a work of fiction. Whilst
places and areas are factual, the characters, incidents and
dialogue within this book are purely fictional and are the
products of the author's imagination. Resemblances to
individuals or events are coincidental and are not to be
construed as real.

Books by the same author

The English Recluse
Susan M Higgins

Oscillate
Susan M Higgins

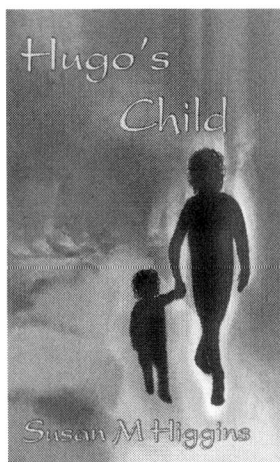

Hugo's Child
Susan M Higgins

4

author's note

The muse's function still flourishes in all areas of society and, whilst the key role of an artist's muse was traditionally reserved for women, there were and still are, many men who have enjoyed and still enjoy the revered role.

An onlooker in yesteryear's society might have perceived the muse as being someone who was beautiful, young, servile, co-dependent and absent of personality; a person who was without a voice and held captive within a genius' stronghold.

However, most muses then were poised and today they still remain confident and intelligent enough to know the power they possess, purely by being a singular source of inspiration.

There is something seductively empowering about being one. Although sexual connotations are often linked to the artist/muse relationship, it doesn't necessarily need to be.

Far from being passive and voiceless, the modern muse influences, inspires and is usually, but not always, equally as ingenious as the artist.

Could it be that the artist defines the muse, or does the muse define the artist?

From a discrete perspective, everyone is capable of being their own muse. When we are self-aware, we can tap into our innate inspiration and create our own aesthetic masterpieces.

*"The mission of an architect is
to help people understand
how to make life more beautiful,
the world a better one for living in and
to give reason, rhyme and meaning to life".*

Frank Lloyd Wright 1957

As always, my thanks are extended to Heather, for her illustrations and her endless patience with me when preparing my work for publication.

Further thanks go to SR and CM for encouraging me to compose this, my fourth novel. Many thanks are also extended to Steve E for proofreading my work.

A final thank you goes to all of my readers, who have generously taken the time to read and review my novels.

Prologue

Following the death of her husband, she decided to return to learning. On achieving a degree in interior design, she opened her own design consultancy. Whilst her life was full on, it was also empty. Empty, in the sense that she longed for that special person to share it with. Following a few meaningless flings, she got lucky.

****

He, a celebrated architect, was still smarting from the after-effects of an acrimonious divorce. Not relishing the idea of reaching retirement without anyone to enjoy it with, he too was searching for a partner to share his life. With a little professional help, his muse appeared.

****

He'd endured much hardship on his arduous journey, to what he thought would be a better life. When he found himself homeless and living on the streets, he never imagined that some kind person would bestow so many opportunities on him and that his life would change completely.

****

Oblivious to the world around him, his addictions led him to a dark place, where he would commit a serious crime. Unexpectedly, he was given another chance to turn his life around and, in doing so, discovered a hidden secret.

one

The driver of the sleek, black Mercedes drove up to the electric gates, leaned out of the window and pressed button 4 on the keypad. The vehicle's air conditioning had been keeping him quite cool, whilst he'd travelled from his previous appointment through the small town of Wilmslow.

Inconveniently, on reaching his journey's end, several beads of perspiration had started to drip down the back of his neck onto the collar of his immaculate white shirt. He inhaled deeply and exhaled slowly.

Aware of the camera pointing directly at him, he patiently waited for the automated security gates to release, before slowly driving onto the secluded, open-plan development. Obviously, she'd seen him arrive on her monitor.

Distracted by what lay before him, he stopped the car; unexpectedly captivated with the four bespoke contemporary structures. All were white, predominantly geometric and deftly constructed of expansive glass facades.

He appreciated the impeccably manicured open-plan frontages, which balanced the atypical setting. The spacious driveways could hold at least six cars, although none were visibly parked.

A high white concrete wall and a grove of tall, structured trees were all positioned around the perimeter, offering plenty protection from unwelcome onlookers and intruders. His uncompromising eye scanned every detail of the enviable gated community.

As the gates closed behind him, he drove slowly past the first house, astutely scanning the large plot of land to the side of it. It was his job to be observant. Always on the lookout for new potential, he shook his head, unable to believe how he hadn't heard about this desirable acreage. It could possibly be about three and a half acres or more. He'd really missed out on this one, big time!

He speculated on which firm of architects had been responsible for designing the stunning structures. Having influenced umpteen emerging designers and, having worked alongside numerous outstanding architects worldwide, his business portfolio was quite extensive.

Images of several distinctive, nonconforming structures flashed through his photographic memory. Try as he might, he was momentarily unable to pinpoint an individual architect; although the houses weren't too dissimilar to the design features of a celebrated Japanese architect, Yoshio Takada, whom he'd worked with on many ambitious developments in the major cities of England and Japan.

Back then, both men were young and sharp, innovative and fearless, ambitious and seeking. Now they were internationally revered architects, having received many awards for their contemporary designs.

Whoever the aficionado may be, she or he certainly had exceptional talent and an advanced insight into design.

It was evident that the developer hadn't been too greedy when planning the lay of the land. Easily, they could have fitted twice as many houses as there were on this plot.

In this affluent stockbroker belt in Cheshire, it was a given that houses of this quality, with substantial space between each dwelling, could command a hefty price.

Unaware that her neighbours' security systems were also able to see him arrive, he turned into the driveway of Number 4, Chancel Quarter and parked his car.

Glancing in the driving mirror, he adjusted his tie and ran his fingers through his steel grey, newly-trimmed hair. Genetics had been especially kind to him. At sixty-four, he was healthy with no known ailments. He was comparatively handsome, or so he'd been informed. Working out most evenings in his home gym, enabled him to keep his slim torso toned and well-defined.

As the CEO of a successful architect practice in the centre of Liverpool, his image was important. He also enjoyed the satisfying feeling of being smartly dressed in Italian and French designer wear.

Stepping out onto the driveway, he adjusted his tie again. Tugging at the shirt cuffs and checking his cuff links, he walked towards the door. He wondered if he looked too formal.

From her photograph, she was a stunner; but then how many stunning photos had he seen? In real life, the women he'd met, were far different than the images they'd uploaded onto their dating profiles. Hopefully, she'd be as beautiful as she appeared to be in her photo and, as interesting as the prolonged dialogues which they'd been exchanging, via texts and phone calls.

He felt that he was ready to be with someone on a permanent basis. It had been just over two years since his wife had left him and he didn't relish the thought of being on his own for the rest of his life. Neither was it his desire to have any more meaningless flings with women, who conveniently satisfied the stirring in his loins, but were only interested in what his position and wealth could offer them.

He wanted more than eye candy on his arm. He craved someone who could touch his soul and make him feel special again.

As she opened the door and stepped out, he was not disappointed.

Dressed casually, but elegantly, in white linen trousers and an open-weaved pale blue jumper, which revealed her lace camisole underneath, she smiled coyly. Her cropped hair was as grey as his was; a natural beauty and exactly like her photograph.

Relieved, he was beyond thankful that she was just as he imagined she would be.

Her unspoken gratitude mirrored his. She'd hoped this one would turn out to be more suitable than her previous dalliances. Whilst they may have been youthful, good looking and undoubtedly virile, they'd lacked substance, flair, intelligence and class. She'd never compromised her safety by bringing them into her home. Her friend had introduced her to some men and was always aware of her whereabouts when she went on dates.

Maybe, the expensive dating agency had finally found a suitable match for her!

"Hello, Alastair. Glad you found it. Come on in."

As he stepped over the threshold, he leant over and pecked her on both cheeks.

"It's so nice to eventually meet you in person."

15

two

As he walked into the open space, the spectacular light-filled interior's clean lines and the white marble floor drew him in. He noticed immediately that the neutral palette was free from any hint of feminine frills or flowery textures. The bold spaces flowed easily into each other and he experienced an instant feeling of calm.

"Would you like to have a look around?"

As she gave him a guided tour, she watched as he surveyed every single measure of floor space, nodding his head and smiling broadly, whilst asking several ambiguous questions; some of which she found difficult to answer. She was familiar with some jargon, but his use of archi-speak baffled her.

A white leather sofa was positioned against the wall on the left and the kitchen area was situated to the right of the space. No appliances and storage areas were visible. All were hidden behind pocket floor to ceiling doors. An expansive island served as a dining surface.

Clearly, the architect had not focused on function over form. Some designers have made that mistake. His own philosophy was that the design of the space needed to be equally as aesthetic, if not more!

Looking towards her, with both of his palms outstretched, he deliberately emphasised every single word, as he eagerly praised the distinctive elements within her house. The architect had Ingeniously developed the bespoke layout to maximise the full potential of the floor space.

"This spatial experience is such an excellent example of simple and subtle sophistication. I like it. I like it a lot."

His preciseness amused her, as he continued nodding his head.

Unexpectedly, she gently pressed her remote keypad and a tri-folding, transparent glass wall opened and then slotted back on itself, into a hidden panel inside the wall.

After examining the irregular mechanisms of the panel, he walked into the garden, commenting further.

"This direct connection between the outside and the inside, gives you a further feeling of space, doesn't it?

"Yes. It really does. I feel more connected with the environment. When I'm upstairs, I can see across the fields and the small cemetery, which has a particularly poignant link to this piece of land. The ancient landed-gentry, who originally resided in The White House as it was known, buried their relatives in a plot of land to the rear of their property. They'd also built a small chantry, but only the foundations remain. If you'd like to come upstairs with me, I'll show you."

Grinning, he speculated on whether her double entendre was intentional. Following her inside, he was tempted to enquire if it was an 'invitation', but he decided against it.

Noting his beaming reaction, she pressed the remote keypad and the folding wall closed.

He deliberated on how the developers had managed to gain planning permission. Contemporary dwellings didn't suit the taste of many Cheshire socialites and, from experience, he knew that most of his clients in this area had preferred the traditional style of house with its antique interior design.

Scanning the open space, he admired a few statement pieces of sculptured art and two oversized, abstract paintings which adorned the stark walls leading up to the half-glazed mezzanine area.

If he hadn't been aware of her occupation, he would have sussed immediately, by her uncluttered approach, that she was a professional. He knew several designers who misunderstand the concept of 'less is more' and she was definitely not of that ilk.

When they reached to top of the white marble staircase, another open space welcomed them into her studio area. Beyond was a second living area, smaller to the one downstairs, but still a sizeable expanse.

He could see now what she meant when she looked out. Through another panelled wall of glass, the sprawling countryside came into his view. Stepping out onto a terraced area, he looked towards the left of her property and saw the ancient remains of the chantry with its sloping gravestones.

Away from her organised workspace, there were four capacious bedrooms, all with en-suites and generous walk-in closets. He appreciated how she'd cleverly used a variety of graphic white textures to add visual impact.

Returning downstairs, they sat opposite each other at a bespoke white quartz island, chatting idly over a light lunch of chicken Caesar salad.

"Who lives in the other houses?"

"Well, the couple who live in Number One own a string of fine dining establishments and some chic bars in Wilmslow, Alderley Edge and Tarporley. He's a three starred Michelin chef and his wife is a lady who lunches, whilst overseeing the financial side of their businesses. They have wonderful dinner parties. Their two children run the business with them."

He thought of how he'd frequented quite a few restaurants and bars in those areas and wondered if he knew them. That might be interesting!

"The couple in Number Two have a successful glazing company. They don't have children."

She took a sip of her elderflower presse and tried to concentrate on his facial gestures.

"The people who live in Number Three own three elite nursing homes in the area. Like me, they also don't have children."

"As you already know, me neither. My wife and I made a decision to concentrate on our careers. The time just flew by. It seemed that I was forever studying; ten years in total and then climbing the corporate ladder. I was so dynamic, passionate and confident. I suppose that's how I gradually acquired my reputation. I knew what I wanted. I went out there and got it. Sometimes, I do regret our decision, but I can't change things."

His vulnerability surfacing, he quickly changed the subject.

"Can I ask you something?"

Wondering what he was going to ask, she raised her eyebrows and pressed her lips.

"What made you choose to buy this specific property?"

His question was easy to answer.

"After Leo died, I wanted to reinvent myself. The house was so empty without him. I wanted to challenge myself and do new things with my life. It

19

wasn't easy. I had to push myself. Anyhow, after I'd qualified in interior design and achieved my degree, one of my clients had told me about the development. I didn't hesitate. I was straight in there. I was very lucky to get this. It was the last one."

"I can see why they sold quickly and the need not to advertise."

"I moved in nine months ago. I'm so content living here, knowing that the neighbours are close by. I lived in a large house in its own grounds before. I was lonely. Here, I'm not. They look out for me. We've all become friends. The people who live here are very hardworking and self-made. They're so different from the other power couples I previously mixed with.

"Where did you live before?"

"About four miles down the road at Prestbury. Here, we sometimes have social gatherings on the lawns or in each other's houses during the winter months."

He could immediately relate with her neighbours' work ethics. He'd also worked hard and earned enough money to provide himself with a good lifestyle. There was nothing improper with people wanting to achieve. Although, he had heard that the area's aristocrats and classic old money weren't too pleased when the swift acceleration of several new money celebrities and sportspeople had filtered into the area decades ago.

Even though the inhabitants of Wilmslow would have liked to believe that they could all live harmoniously in the renowned Golden Triangle, it just wasn't the case.

More than one of his clients had told him that the upper class sedate lifestyle had been disturbed and they'd openly voiced their utter disapproval, on more than one occasion.

Despite their disfavour, the new money folk were content with becoming part of the 'Cheshire Set'. Displaying their conspicuous consumption on a lavish scale, they'd firmly placed Cheshire on the fiscal map.

Esme could have bought any house she'd wanted, but this was the house she'd chosen. Part of her substantial inheritance, from her late husband's estate, had paid for it. The purchase hadn't even made a slight dent in her eight figure assets, which included three investment properties.

"That sounds nice."

Impressed with the unified look which had been created throughout the house, his thoughts returned to the architect who'd been responsible for designing the houses.

"I really do like it here. I must admit, these houses are not too dissimilar to my own signature blend; contemporary, sophisticated and, much more importantly, sustainable. Do you have the name of the architect who designed them?"

"I do somewhere. It'll be on the plans. I'll find it for you and message you."

He looked at his watch. He'd arranged another appointment, just in case she wasn't the person he'd expected her to be. Fortunately, his clients didn't live that far away. He regretted it now. He'd have liked to stay longer.

"Awh! Sorry. I hadn't noticed the time. I have an appointment in Knutsford at 3.00. I'd better go."

Presuming he was going to be spending the afternoon with her, she was disappointed.

As he left the house, he looked around for her

car.

"Hey. Where do you keep your car?"

She went inside and retrieved the remote. As she pressed the pad, a concealed opening resembling part of the house's structure, raised to reveal her black Lexus SUV.

"Impressed?"

"Very impressed. Clever aesthetics. So that's the reason I didn't see any cars on the driveways?"

As previously, he moved closer and kissed her lightly on both cheeks.

"Bye. Thanks again for lunch. Don't forget to let me have the name of the architect."

As she watched him approach the gates, she pressed her remote to open them, thrilled that he'd reached his arm out of the car window to wave to her.

Again, he eyed up the spacious plot at the side of the first house. If he could buy that land, he could design an amazing house and make a tidy profit in the process.

Returning inside, she didn't know what to think. Was he interested? Would there be another date? Did he like her? Although she'd sensed a palpable energy flowing between them, she wasn't sure. He hadn't said that he'd ring her.

She ran upstairs, switched on her computer and opened the 'house' file. Locating the correct document, she clicked on it and found the architect's name. After typing the details into his message box, she quickly pressed the send button.

As an afterthought, she questioned whether she'd been too eager in forwarding the details.

"Well, Esme Clarke, you're quite taken with him, aren't you?"

three

As he drove to his appointment, instead of preparing his thoughts for his next client, his mind was solely preoccupied with her. He'd seen something in her that he respected. Yes, he liked her. He liked her house. He liked the satisfying interior atmosphere which she'd created. The dynamic way in which she conceptualised informal space, was so similar to his.

Before going into his client's premises, he'd been tempted to message her, just to thank her again, but thought against it. Switching off his phone, he rang the doorbell.

After a successful two-hour session with a young couple who were interested in building their own home, he'd taken several notes and was sure he could design them a stunning residence. They'd given him a fairly-free rein to do what he wanted, so long as sustainable materials were used in its construction, it was cost effective and environmentally friendly.

It was only when he entered his own house, that he switched on his phone. Scrolling quickly through his messages, he was elated to see a voice message from her. He clicked on it.

"I really have enjoyed our time together today, Alastair. Thanks for coming."

He then noticed the text containing the name of the architect. He hadn't heard of him.

Should he ring her? He decided to text her instead.

'Thanks for your voice message and the text. I

did too. I love your home. Looking forward to seeing you again – that's if you want to? X'

He pressed the send button and waited. Sure enough, a reply came.

'That would be lovely. Me too. Enjoy your evening. X'

He placed some chicken and vegetables in the oven to roast. His mind was racing, his pulse was racing, he couldn't stop thinking about her. During the time he'd been speaking to her on the phone before they met, he felt that she'd already crept into his head and made herself comfortable. He had to admit that he was comfortable with her being there, but it was somewhat distracting.

Whilst waiting for his meal to cook, he spent half an hour in the gym. Exercise always made him feel better after a day's work. He focused his mind on the young couple's specification and visualised what the finished design would look like. Some would say his designs were rigid and cold. That was their opinion and they were entitled to it.

He increased the resistance on his exercise bike and pedalled for three minutes, before reducing it again.

Returning to his previous ponderings, he believed his approach was constantly evolving. He'd designed for various settings and situations, including many period properties, but he had a preferred style and there was nothing wrong with that.

After showering, he sat at the table pushing the food around his plate. He knew he was falling; fast! The fluttering sensations in his stomach were a warning sign.

"Just eat your meal", he admonished himself.

Placing his plate and glass in the dishwasher, he made his way upstairs.

Ping. He opened his phone. It was from her.

'Goodnight. Sleep well. X'

'You, too. X'

Subconsciously, he questioned himself.

"Alastair Brickman. What's got into you? Are you moving too quickly here? Take it easy, man."

He'd been on the verge of falling asleep before he'd received the text. Now, he'd never get to sleep, thinking about her.

four

Having had a restless night, reflecting on his visit, she'd risen at six. She had some work to complete, but her concentration span was limited.

In the centre of her studio, a large table was covered with the tools of her trade. Fabric samples and paint colour swatches were lined up at one end. Several post it notes, a tape measure, sketches, a mood board and a 3D plan were also neatly organised on the large worksurface.

On another smaller table, a large retina display screen housed specialised computer software to assist with the drawings, designing and scheduling of her commissions. As a solopreneur, she managed every element of her business. She preferred it that way; everything in order and only her being in control.

She'd rented a large space within an award-winning, leading design furniture showroom, where she was able to show her clients a fully realised floor plan of their future living space. It had proved to be beneficial, not only for her, but also the showroom. Her clients loved the virtual and interactive design reveal which showcased her sensuous appreciation of colours, shapes, contrast and textures. They were also encouraged to browse through fresh designs and the 'one of a kind' pieces that were displayed throughout the premises. Business was booming for both parties.

Her extensive network of professional and personal connections, who'd freely recommended her design services, were worth more than their weight in gold. Some of the names in her databank included the wives of footballers and other celebrities. They were a competitive bunch – all vying to outdo each other. She wasn't the only interior designer in the area. There were several. However, her reputation for providing tasteful design, preceded her. What they weren't aware of, was that her job was only a hobby for her. The money was irrelevant.

Nevertheless, she was only as good as her last job and it was her punctilious, ethical approach to her work which had enabled her enterprise to flourish. New commissions were scheduled and most of her clients were prepared to wait until she was free to do work for them.

She went downstairs to fetch some water. Dropping a few slices of lime into the glass, she grabbed a banana and an apple before returning upstairs and forcing herself to continue with her work. An afternoon meeting with a client had been arranged and she needed to have everything ready. This individual had already been somewhat difficult; unable to make any definite decisions. Esme had changed the floor plan and textiles several times, only for the client to revert to the original design. It was par for the course. She'd expected it. Despite the challenges, she loved every aspect of her job. Meeting people, being creative and seeing the satisfied look on her clients' faces brought her joy.

Her mind drifted to him, again. Whilst he had openly flirted with her previously, over the telephone, this time he'd adopted the perfect gentleman role; albeit with a twinkle in his eye. She sensed that he was holding back and his formality, during conversation, had made her feel unsure. She pondered on whether he'd call her again.

Quickly brought out of her daydreaming state by a text coming through, she glanced at her watch. It was 1.30pm. She had an hour before she needed to leave, to make sure she arrived at the showroom for 3.00pm.

There hadn't been much traffic on the roads and she'd arrived for her appointment with twenty minutes to spare.

Her meeting had produced results. Her client loved the virtual tour and was now ready to sign off the approval. She was eager for Esme to start the job as soon as was possible.

Juggling several commissions was challenging, considering she'd recently had to dispense with the services of one of her best workers. He'd been her last fling. She'd known that was never a good thing to mix business with pleasure, but he had initiated the relationship and she couldn't resist his charms. He was twenty-five years younger and as 'fit as fuck'; as her friend had crudely informed her.

Whilst it had been exciting at the beginning, she had to admit that she couldn't keep up with him. He had become far too demanding, physically and otherwise. He had wanted to party all the time. She wanted to sleep. He'd wanted to control her. That was never going to happen. She'd ended it. Pronto!

She'd learned her lesson the hard way. Due to taking her 'eye of the ball', she'd felt humiliated when she'd nearly lost her client. Fortunately, she was given another chance and had managed to get back on track, by throwing herself into her work. She'd also managed to engage the services of another reliable tradesman.

As she opened the front door, her phone rang. Dropping her portfolio and laptop onto the floor, she rummaged through the bottom of her bag to find it, hoping it wouldn't go off before she could locate it. She hoped it would be him.

"Hi. I left you a message earlier. Did you get it?"

"Hi. No, my phone's been on silent and I haven't checked it. Sorry."

"Was just wondering if you wanted to join me for dinner, later."

"Yes. I'd love to join you. What time were you thinking?"

Her mind was racing, thinking about what she'd wear and if she'd have enough time to get ready.

"7.30 ok?"

"Look forward to it. See you later."

She looked down at her watch. 6.00pm. She'd better get a move on.

After depositing her work in the studio, she went into her bedroom and stripped off. What was she going to wear? Something cool. It was too hot to wear a fitted dress. She decided on a cobalt blue linen shift; a timeless designer piece which she'd purchased twenty odd years ago from a couturier in Paris. Luxury didn't date.

Once she'd showered, she renewed her make up. These days she preferred the natural look. It was better for her complexion and didn't accentuate her wrinkles. A flash of cerise lip gloss and a generous spray of Tom Ford Neroli Portofino and she was nearly ready.

The buzzer sounded. He was here. Stepping quickly into her dress, she pressed the button to

29

unlock the security gate and grabbed her clutch bag. Her shoes were at the side of the door, ready to step into.

With heart racing and flushed face, she waited for him to arrive before opening the door.

Handing her a simple bunch of flowers, he leant over and, this time, he kissed her firmly on her lips He wanted to. She wanted him to.

He was dressed casually in some navy chinos and a pale blue, chambray shirt, rolled up to his elbows. Seeing the hairs on his forearms, she glanced to see if his chest would be the same. It was. She noticed the way his shirt fitted his slim torso and the way it was tucked into his trousers. She disliked the way some men left their shirts loose, even though she knew that some men preferred it. Polo shirts and tee shirts were ok, but not a buttoned up one.

He opened the car door for her and as they drove to the restaurant, he pressed the touchscreen on the dashboard. She smiled as Andrea Bocelli's unique vocal chords pervaded the car's interior.

She liked his versatile blend of opera and pop music; particularly the symphony he'd sung with Ed Sheeran and when he'd sang with Celine Dion.

No sooner had she thought it, Alastair winked at her and as he accompanied Bocelli's voice, several shivers scuttled down her spine.

Halfway through the song, he stopped singing and allowed Bocelli to continue.

"Well, that was a surprise. You have an amazing voice."

"Thanks. I love to sing his songs. He has such a fabulous range."

Making a mental note of another commonality

they shared, she'd be vigilant. She was certain she'd be adding more to her list!

five

Over dinner, the conversation was flowing, if not the wine.

He wanted to know more about her. She was pleased to furnish him with information.

"As I've previously told you, my husband passed away. I met Leo in an upmarket hotel, where I was having a drink after work with some friends. We seemed to click right away. He had a great Irish sense of humour and he was such a kind, true gentleman. He lived in the outskirts of Dublin, but he had several businesses in England and he also travelled back and forth. I discovered he was twenty years older than me, but that wasn't a problem for either of us. The experience of just being with him was so amazing."

She stopped to eat some of her beetroot-cured sea trout, before continuing.

"Coincidentally, every time I happened to be in the bar having a drink, he was there too. I don't know if I went in hoping to see him, or he went in hoping to see me! I suppose there was a strong connection from the start. I soon felt that it was developing into more than a friendly relationship. The moment I found out he was married, I was disappointed, but when he explained that his wife had cheated on him and left him, I felt that maybe there could be a chance for us to be together."

When he heard the words 'cheated on him and left him', he placed his knife and fork on the side of his plate, took a deep breath and sipped some water.

"I always looked about ten years younger than my age. On several occasions, I was refused a drink in the pubs, because they thought I was underage."

He laughed, but he could see why. At sixty-two, her clear complexion and her fine lines only served to accentuate her natural beauty.

"When we went away for short breaks, the receptionists would assume that we were father and daughter. They'd ask if we required separate rooms. Nine months later, following Leo's acrimonious divorce from his wife, we got married in Cyprus."

He rolled his eyes. Acrimonious divorces were painful on the pocket, as well as the heart.

"We had some superb holidays in the Bahamas, Thailand, France and other countries. He introduced me to numerous celebrities. We were involved in several fundraising events and attended many charity balls. My life changed completely."

Imagining her in her evening dresses, waltzing around the room with her husband, he wondered if he'd have the same opportunity to dance with her.

"He was such an altruistic man. He donated a substantial amount of funding to a women's refuge in Ireland and other charities."

Realising that she hadn't stopped talking, she finished eating her meal.

"Anyhow. How about you?"

"No, you finish. I'm really interested in what you have to say."

Smiling, she continued once more.

"We loved Cyprus so much. Leo retired and I finished work. We moved over there. We designed our own home and were involved in the construction of it. Then we bought another plot and did the same again. We only moved back to England when he became ill."

She reached into her bag for a tissue and wiped her cheek. Talking about him had brought back some blissful memories and some sad ones also. When Leo had been taken from her, she'd perpetually questioned why. His dementia-related illnesses had been painful for them both. From being an intelligent and sharp businessman, he'd become someone unrecognisable, except for episodes when he would whisper endearing comments as she was tending to his needs.

Her pain had given her the courage to venture into something new. She hadn't realised at the time that her pain was to become her strength.

"I nursed him until the end, holding his hand as he passed away. I never thought I'd cope, but I had to. After six months or so, I decided that I needed to do something with my life. There's only so much crying you can do. I was still young. When I was in my thirties, I'd worked as a design coordinator for an exhibition centre. As I was driving into Manchester one afternoon, I saw a sign advertising university courses and when I returned home, I did some research and enrolled on a three-year, full time interior design programme at the reputable Manchester Metropolitan University. I then did a year's placement with a design company on the outskirts of the city. From there, I opened my own consultancy and the rest is history."

In the space of less than an hour, she'd exposed most of her vulnerabilities and also her enduring strengths.

Whenever she spoke about him, her mind

would wander to the photograph of him, leaning over and kissing her. He'd adored her and had always told her so. He'd never left home without kissing her goodbye.

"Your turn, Alastair. Tell me something about your life."

"Well. Where do I start? As a child, I was always interested in buildings. I used to build a line of houses with Lego and pretend it was my own village. If it didn't look right, I'd demolish it and build it again until I was satisfied with it. I suppose the kids use Minecraft now to do that on their computers."

They did! For a while, her friend's son had quite an obsession with the game.

"I've designed quite a few houses around here, in the stockbroker belt, for some footballers and several actors. I didn't use Lego or Minecraft though", he joked.

Smiling, she wondered if he'd designed some of the houses where she'd also undertaken a few commissions.

"I'm part of a small forum which is helping with the construction of various sustainable homes for the future. Along with two other architects, we've offered free advice and our expertise to three couples who are willing to participate in self-build projects."

"That sounds interesting. Which stage are they at?"

"Oh! We're only at the design stage. I've been working with one couple and my colleagues are working with the other two. I've already completed the initial information gathering."

"I married when I was thirty-five. I was too busy studying for qualifications before that; ten years

35

in all. I then worked my arse off, setting up my own consultancy in 1988. I amassed my fortune over the years, through hard slog and sheer determination. I loved my work. I still do; perhaps too much! When I was building my business, I was ruthless. I thrived on chasing deals and clinching them. It was exciting. I carved out a niche for myself. My contemporary designs were 'out there' and I had shedloads of commissions from self-builders and prestigious major corporates."

Her smiled widened. She secretly admired his honest arrogance and work ethic.

"I will admit, at times, I've been disappointed with my some of my protégés. When I was mentoring them, they were too scared to push the boundaries and take risks. I'm sure they thought I was a hard taskmaster and a work addict. I suppose I was, but I wanted to stretch their talent and they couldn't hack it. I've brought out the best in several innovative designers, though. They've moved on to do greater things."

She could see that his self-discipline had been learnt from an early age.

"My wife had decided that she didn't want to work and, whilst I was away in Japan on business, she was tempted by the charms of an attractive young stud. She even owned up to having sex with him in our marital bed. The audacity of her. She made the excuse that she was lonely and that it had only happened a few times. If she was lonely, why the hell did she finish work?"

Esme raised her eyebrows and flinched. She'd done exactly the same with a young man; the only difference being that she was free to do so and it didn't happen in her own bed.

"She'd given me the impression that our marriage was working. I had no reason to think otherwise. Everything she asked for, I gave her. We'd go on exotic holidays. She knew I had to travel with my job. It was my job, for God's sake. I suppose I did have an idea something was going on when she wasn't responsive to my advances. She'd make excuses that she was tired. I must have been gullible not to see what was going on."

He caught the waiter's eye and ordered some more drinks.

"Perrier for me, please. Another wine for you. Esme?"

"Yes, Please."

She was beginning to get a better picture of what kind of a person he was. She loved the way he rested his hand on his chin when he was listening to her and the way he turned his head slightly when he agreed with her.

"Where was I? Oh yes. I tried to forgive her, but I couldn't at the time. Throughout my marriage, I'd never once been unfaithful to my wife, except for a quick Christmas kiss in the pub when I was with my mates. I've been tempted on several occasions, but I've always respected my marriage vows."

He poured water into his glass and raised a toast.

"To us. Let's see what the future brings."

She thought his toast sounded promising.

"At first, I felt as if I wasn't enough and I had a few weeks feeling hurt and rejected. I got drunk a few times, but I soon realised it wasn't that great for my work, or my reputation. I just focused on increasing my business and took on more staff to cope with the influx. We agreed that she'd keep the house as part of the divorce settlement. She wanted it that way. I really loved that house, but hey, it's only bricks and mortar at the end of the day. Thankfully, I'm glad to say that there weren't any children involved. I wouldn't have wanted them to suffer."

He turned around to see a group of women entering the restaurant. She'd glimpsed them too and hoped they hadn't noticed her.

"Afterwards, I had a few opportunist sexual encounters. I'm not proud of it, but it satisfied a need and I always used protection."

He thought he'd mention that. He didn't want her to think he was just having sex with anyone and everyone.

"Looks like we have a few members of the Cheshire Set here on a girl's night out."

Although glamorous in their own way, with their pouting lips and excessive bling, he compared them to Esme and deemed her to be far more sophisticated.

She nodded and shrugged her shoulders. Having finished their meal, she thought of how they could manage to escape before the girls spotted her.

The other diners' heads weren't turned. They were used to seeing them in their figure hugging dresses, which revealed their heaving cleavages, their dazzling white teeth and perfectly manicured talons.

It was evident, by their perfect tans and make up, that they'd been for a full day's pampering at one of the beauty salons. She'd been with them on a few occasions. She knew they could appear to be a bit over the top, but they'd befriended her when she was lonely. There was no harm in them. Esme had first met one of the women when she was commissioned to redesign some rooms in her home. She'd been grateful for her friendship and, when she wasn't working into the early hours of the morning completing a project, she'd spend the evening with them.

Esme heard one of the girls ordering a bottle of Tattinger Prestige Rose and she wondered how many glasses of pink fizz they'd downed already. .

Having never really bought into all of that celebrity stuff, she now preferred a simple life; similar to the one she'd had when she was growing up as an only child.

Even though she was financially comfortable, she knew she'd have been able to survive if she had to.

"Shall we leave now? It's getting a bit rowdy in here."

She was so glad he'd asked.

"Yes. That's a good idea."

Before the waiter had brought the bill, they'd been spotted. The skimpily clad women came tottering over to the table, trying not to spill the sparkling liquid in their flutes.

"Hi, Esme. What are you doing in here? We haven't seen you for ages. Are you ok?"

"Hi. Yes, thanks."

Another girl answered the question.

"You can see what she's doing in here. Having a meal with her new fella."

As Alastair took charge of the situation, Esme's face reddened as the giggling women were becoming louder.

"Nice to have met you all. Sorry, we're just leaving."

"Awh! Don't go yet. Stay and talk with us."

"We need to be somewhere, soon", he replied.

"Esme. Don't forget to give us a call. We've all missed you."

As they walked back towards the car, he smiled.

"How do you know them?"

"I've done some work in their houses and I've been out with them a few times."

"I bet you had some fun."

She nodded. She had. She'd explain later.

After inviting him in for a coffee, they talked some more and embraced. He forced himself to leave. If he'd stayed any longer, he'd be tempted to take it further and he knew it wasn't the right thing to do.

"I think it's time for me to leave now."

His phone rang. He looked at it and let it ring.

He kissed her again at the door and, as she watched him walk to his car, she was tempted to go after him and touch his taut bum. His close-fitting trousers, revealing his toned thighs, had aroused her. As he turned around and winked at her, her heart skipped a beat.

On his way home, he pondered on whether it would be possible to woo her slowly. Not only was she intriguing; she was also quite attractive. He'd had to stop himself from enticing her earlier!

six

The following day, after asking his personal assistant to do some digging around on the internet, Alastair discovered that the architect had originally hailed from Edinburgh.

Having lived and worked in Japan for five years, he'd recently married the great granddaughter of the aristocrat who had owned the sprawling white house and outbuildings, which had originally been sited on the plot.

The ancient properties had been left to fall into disrepair. Not wanting to live in a crumbling mansion or to be responsible for the renovation of it, the remaining members of the family had gone to live in warmer climes.

Due to the unsafe condition of the buildings, permission had been granted for the properties to be demolished and four substantial detached dwellings to be erected in their place.

The only stipulation being, that the graveyard and the remains of the ancient chantry would stay.

It had been a fantastic opportunity for the young designer to make his mark in England.

Chancel Quarter was put on the map.

Armed with a handful of drawings and some documents, he'd take great pleasure in sifting through them later.

seven

He'd been out of the country for eight days, at a design exhibition in Germany. Whilst there, he'd sourced some building materials for the self-build project.

Although they'd facetimed a couple of times and texted each other, he'd missed her. Throughout their conversations, each had been figuring out where the relationship was going.

During the day time, Esme had been kept occupied, completing three rooms in a period property in Alderley Edge.

In the evenings, after a glass of wine, she'd even fantasised about him, visualising what he'd look like naked. He looked quite fit in his clothes and she was sure he'd look equally as fit without them!

She awoke at six. He was coming to collect her later. Trying to pass the time, she made a smoothie and flicked through some of her rough drawings. Her preoccupied thoughts of him flooded her flustered brain and she couldn't settle to do anything.

At 11.00am precisely, the buzzer from the security gate sounded and she let him in. As the car pulled onto the drive, she could hardly breathe as she opened the front door. She just wanted to see his face and hold him.

"Hello Es. How are you doing?"

Her face lit up when she saw him.

"I'm good, thank you."

He placed his suit bag and an overnight bag over the sofa. Anticipating what was to come, the corners of her lips raised slightly and her cheeks flushed.

Closing the door, he took her in his arms and hugged her. Then he planted several meaningful kisses on her pouting lips.

"I've missed you, Es. It seems ages since I last saw you."

"Me too."

He had an overwhelming urge to make love to her, but they'd planned to go to the Artisan Market in Wilmslow and he wanted the first time with her to be special and unrushed.

Later, after they'd bought foodstuffs for their meal, they'd cook dinner together.

In the car, on the way there, they chatted incessantly.

As well as buying fresh salmon and vegetables, they also bought a bottle of ginger and rhubarb gin, chilli and lime chutney, Cheshire cheese, oat biscuits, green olives, sundried tomatoes and braised garlic bulbs.

They managed to locate a seat at the rear of a small café on the high street and, after eating a light lunch, they were surprised when a lady asked if she could sit with them.

With raised eyebrows, they looked at each other and nodded.

"Please do", he replied.

Whilst she opened her coat and made herself comfortable, the waitress lingered before placing a tray with a pot of tea and a scone in front of her.

"Hello lovies. Thanks for letting me sit with you. I'm Edith, but you can call me Edi if you want to. What's your names?"

"I'm Alastair and this is Esme."

She buttered her warm scone and spread the jam thickly onto it, before taking a generous bite.

"Years ago, this village was very different from what it is today. It was great here in the forties and fifties. We had some fun, dancing and courting. I met my husband at a dance."

She took a sip of her tea and another bite of the scone.

They both smiled, waiting for her to continue.

"Hey, all these new money folk just want the prestige of living here, but you never see them getting involved in any of the activities. The ordinary folk in the village and surrounding areas were a bit starstruck at first when those footballers came. They bought up some of the big houses and some started building those massive mansions. It was never heard of in my days. Loads of money for kicking a ball up and down a field. What's that all about? Someone told me one footballer gets paid £8.3 million a month. It's stupid money, isn't it?"

They all laughed.

"I know you're laughing at me, but it's true. The world's gone mad."

They listened to her personal perspective. That's all she wanted – someone to listen. She lived on her own in a terraced house just outside the village. Her family had wanted to put her in a nursing home. She was having none of it.

"I also told them that the only way they'll get me out of my home is in a wooden box. I'm going nowhere. I said that if they did that to me, they wouldn't get any of my inheritance. It would all go to the nursing home, wouldn't it?"

She chuckled again and they laughed with her.

"I'm not lonely, you know. You don't need to feel sorry for me. I read lots of books and I still bake my own bread and cakes. I just come here to keep in touch with what's going on in the village. I could tell you a story or two about this place. I could write a book!"

Alastair encouraged her.

"You ought to, Edi. It would make interesting reading."

"No. I couldn't. I'd get too many people into trouble. Although some of those who I could write about have died. They were womanisers. Having flings with other women and then the women having their babies. The wives were bloody stupid. Once the men got fed up, they'd go back to their wives crying and begging for forgiveness. The women would take them back. What else could they do? They'd nowhere else to go, with the loads of kids their husbands had given them. They had to stay put. The men were bringing the money in and putting food on the table."

She was quiet for a moment and seemed distant.

His phone rang and he cut the call, bringing Edi back into the conversation.

"Oh, ay! It was different in those days. We had it rough and the women before us. Men thought it was their God-given right to control and be worshipped. Some of you women have it easy these days. You have good jobs and you don't need a man to look after you. There was none of this women's lib stuff, like there is these days. We put up and shut up. The men thought we didn't know that they still couldn't keep it in their pants, especially when they'd been chatting up the

45

barmaids and the WAAF's in the pubs."

She poured more tea into her cup and added some milk. Stirring it continuously, she tapped the spoon on the edge of the cup three times.

"Do you know something? I wish I'd been born later than I was. I'd have joined those women's libbers and burnt my bra. I'd have left the cheating bastard, too. I'd have educated myself and got a good job."

Edi chortled and they laughed with her.

"There used to be a picture house over there, but it closed in 1955. We had some great times there, kissing and cuddling on the back row."

Fascinated, they patiently waited for her next disclosure.

"Hey, I don't know if you've heard that Alan Turing lived here. He was the Nazi code breaker in World War Two. He lived in Adlington Road. I bet you didn't know that, did you?"

They did know, but they allowed her to have her moment and shook their heads.

"Well, he did. They've done his house up now. If you walk past it, you'll know which one it is. There's one on them signs outside."

Reverting to her previous conversation, Edi continued.

"Like I say, I could write a bloody book. I should know. My kids have at least three half-siblings that I know of and they didn't live that far away from us either. They were in school together. The teacher used to ask them if they were cousins. Not bloody cousins! Blood sisters and brothers! I knew they were his. They were the spitting image of him. He couldn't deny them, but he did!"

Tipping the cup, she drained the dregs of tea.

Scraping the last few crumbs of scone from her plate, she licked her fingers before continuing once more.

"In 1947, my husband was stationed in the RAF in Number Four in Wilmslow. He'd trained all the new recruits before they went away to war. They demolished the building in 1962 and they've built some big houses on it now. He was a handsome chap. It's no wonder all the ladies were after him."

Bowing her head, she pulled a handkerchief from out of her pocket. Pretending to blow her nose, she wiped her cheek.

"Oh! Edi. We've had such a lovely time talking to you."

"Have you love? It's been lovely talking to both of you, too."

Throwing back her head, she chuckled loudly.

"Although, I think I have done most of the talking, haven't I?"

They laughed with her.

"Well, I'd better be going now. Hey, I'd better not forget to pay my bill. They'll soon be after me."

"Have this one on us, Edi."

She leant over and grabbed his hand and then held onto Esme's.

"Thanks, lovies. You've both made my day. I do hope I see you again. Look out for me, won't you?"

"We will, Edi. We will", they replied in unison.

Both watched as she went to the counter and the waitress looked over.

Alastair lifted his hand in acknowledgement. As she shuffled out of the café, she turned around, waved her hand and blew them a kiss.

"Well, wasn't she a character? A wonderful lady. Sounds as if she's had a hard life. She took us on

47

a trip down memory lane, didn't she?"

"Oh! She did. She's given us a glimpse into what some of the villagers are thinking as well."

"Her husband seemed to be quite fond of the ladies."

"So it seemed. I wonder if she really loved him, or just stayed with him because she didn't have any alternative."

He raised his eyebrows.

"She may tell us next time. I hope we see her again. I'd love to hear more of her tales."

"I really liked her. She was so down to earth. I wonder where she lives. She didn't actually say, did she?"

"I think we'd better go ourselves. We'll be stuck in traffic and never get out of the village when the stallholders start packing up."

On the way home they chatted about Edi again.

"I do hope she got home ok". When she told us her age, I couldn't help but think that she'd be around the same age as my husband would have been now. I hope you don't mind me talking about him. He was a gentle gentleman. He used to tell me tales of when he was younger and, when she told us some of her history, I couldn't help but recollect our times together."

"Don't be silly, Esme. Why would I mind? He was a big part of your life. We're home now. I'd love to hear more about him."

He stopped the car on the driveway and leant over. Placing his hand on her chin, he lifted her face toward his, positioned his lips on her and kept them there.

She never thought her heart would heal after losing Leo. The way this man had just kissed her, she thought that he might just be able to heal it!

eight

That evening, after dinner, he proceeded to tell her about a project he'd initiated.

"I originally thought of the idea after I'd met a homeless man sheltering in a doorway in Dale Street, not too far from my office. It was raining and the stale smell of damp clothes and body odour hit me as I walked past him. He wasn't begging. He didn't even have an empty container for donations. He was just sat there, sad and dishevelled."

"What did you do?"

"The pain in his eyes really got to me. His face haunted me as I carried on walking. Whilst buying my own lunch, I bought him some too and, on my way back, I stopped and spoke with him. He was shivering and he kept pulling a dirty threadbare blanket around his shoulders. His worldly goods were stored in two plastic supermarket bags. I gave him the sandwich and a drink of hot chocolate and he started to cry. He thanked me profusely and called me Sir."

"How awful for him. He called you Sir?"

"Yes. I told him not to and that my name was Alastair. He said his name was Ali and that he'd seen me walking past a few times. I have to admit, I'm always in a rush and I'd never noticed him before."

Listening intently, she thought how it was so easy to turn your head and walk past another human being who was suffering. She'd done the same on a few occasions, but the person didn't want food. They only wanted money. Not wanting to feed their habit by giving them cash, she'd just left the food with them. It had been difficult to know what to do. Maybe, they'd wanted it to buy toiletries. She hadn't even thought to ask.

"Do you think society has become desensitised to seeing people living a subhuman existence on the streets?"

"I do. Yes. Anyhow, I discovered that Ali was a refugee from Syria. He'd been staying with his cousin, but after a disagreement, he'd been asked to leave. He'd tried to find somewhere to live, but without success. He wasn't a user of substances or dependent on alcohol. He just didn't have anywhere to live."

Raising her eyebrows, she rested her hands under her chin.

"I needed to get back for a meeting, so I folded up a ten-pound note and placed it in his hand. He began crying again, thanking me profusely in his fractured English accent."

She lowered her head slightly.

"I repeated that he shouldn't call me by that name. He just smiled and said he would call me Ali Sir because it was nearly the same as Alastair."

They both smiled.

"I do know that an element of the Syrian culture is to be respectful to their elders. He was so grateful. When I'd finished work, I felt compelled to see him again, but he wasn't there. Throughout the evening, I couldn't get him out of my mind."

Intrigued to know more, she questioned him.

"Did you see him the following day?"

"Yes. He was with another man, who was propped up against the doorway. The stale stench of

51

alcohol oozed out of him and he moved away when I stopped to talk with Ali, although I was fully aware that he was eavesdropping on our conversation."

Attentively listening, she replenished his now empty glass.

"He told me that he'd been kicked by a passer-by on several occasions when he'd been sleeping in the doorway at night. Afterwards, he was frightened to sleep, in case he was attacked again. Some people had even thrown buckets of water over him and other homeless substance users had held him down and rifled through his pockets for drugs and money."

"Oh! It's dreadful, Alastair."

"Ali said that his friend, the man who had walked away, had always fought them off. They shared their food and money with each other and talked about their troubles. He also told me that his friend was alcohol dependent and a substance user."

"At least he had someone to look out for him. Did you ever think that Ali might be an illegal refugee?"

"Yes, I did. When I asked him, he showed me his immigration papers. They were folded up in a small plastic bag and he kept them hidden under his several layers of clothes. He has permission to stay. He's legit."

She wondered how he would have reacted if he'd discovered that Ali was an illegal immigrant.

"I didn't want to pry too much about his life before he came to England. He told me snippets about some of his darkest moments and it was enough for me to see the bigger picture. He had witnessed brutality and unspeakable violence and how he was used to being cold, sleeping in flooded fields and being desperately hungry. I could sense his misery and his fragile heart, when he spoke about his family who were still living in the refugee camps. He was ashamed to be living on the streets, but he was also glad that he was living in an area where people didn't recognise him."

Alastair silently reflected for a moment on Ali's predicament. Why did some people think it was ok to abuse the homeless? He'd read about numerous homeless entrepreneurs, who'd constructed fake identities to make money and then went home to a comfortable house. Ali had also told him that homeless people regarded each other as family, but there was definitely a hierarchy in the street communities.

"He believes in fate and he feels that he is living in England for a reason. He says whatever is going to happen will happen anyway."

"He sounds a nice man. So, what's your idea, then?"

"Well, I've spoken with a lawyer friend and some other philanthropists about doing something to get the vulnerable people off the streets. One of them owns a run-down building in the city centre, at the back of Bold Street. He said they could use it free of charge, but it needed some renovation."

"That's sounds great. So where are you up to with it?"

"We've been having talks with other business owners, to see if they'd get involved and we've had a good response. All of them have donated substantial amounts of money and have offered their services free of charge. I'm meeting with them next week, to finalise how we're going to make it happen and to estimate a completion date. It'll provide interim term accommodation and also offer different types of rehabilitation support, to help with their recovery."

She gazed deeply into his eyes and her own Nunchi* immediately identified with his extremely sensitive ability to judge and respond to others' feelings. After partaking in several lengthy telephone conversations and, only having met him just three times, his altruistic nature was just one of his many attractive attributes.

Further contemplating on how Alastair's heart had spiritually spoken to him, urging him to help those needy individuals who were enduring homelessness, she discerned that Ali had been the catalyst. His willing vision to help the homeless touched her own heart and, as she held her hand below her left breast, she could feel it pumping furiously.

She thought about Article 14 of the Human Rights Declaration which justly states that everyone has the right to be accepted everywhere as a person, according to law and everyone should have access to adequate food, water, sanitation, clothing and housing. She wondered where the homeless went to wash themselves and their clothes.

*Nunchi means soul – a form of emotional intelligence.

nine

Digging his thumbs into the top of his pockets, he leant against the wall and watched her as she prepared the rhubarb and ginger dessert. He had an irresistible urge to reach out and touch her.

Sensing he was observing her, she slowly turned around. Smiling, she noted his sexual stance.

After they'd eaten, they cuddled on the sofa, listening to Debussy's Suite Bergamasque and some other of his timeless masterpieces.

Although she'd enjoyed Prelude, Menuet and Passepied, it was the soothing Clair de lune melody which had initially hooked her. Its mysterious and complex chords resonated with the way she had felt then and how she'd been feeling of late.

Whilst the peaceful melody soothed her, it also provoked sentimental reflections within her, as it echoed around the voluminous space.

Leaning against his chest, she began to recite the first line of the French poet, Verlaine's famous work, 'Your soul is a chosen landscape'.

He raised his eyebrows as she proceeded with her confident recital.

Comparing her own interpretation of the poem to the poet's depiction, she also blurred the boundaries between what was real and what was imaginary in her life. Visualising someone taking away her sadness and making her feel alive again, she yearned for a lover to dance with her in the magical moonlight.

It was a given that he'd stay the night. The exchange of sexual innuendoes over the past few weeks and the continuous verbal foreplay during the evening, had whet their appetites. The copious amounts of champagne had also steered them along.

It seemed so natural for them to take their relationship to the next level.

After the second bottle had been emptied, he took her hand and guided her upstairs, kissing her on the way.

She'd been waiting weeks for this. She was going to enjoy it. The build-up to it had been exciting, yet somewhat frustrating.

Not needing any encouragement, she quickly stepped out of her dress. Loving the sensual feeling of nakedness, she'd purposely not worn any underwear.

His enlarged pupils were on stalks, as he slowly absorbed every inch of her slender form. He hadn't realised that she'd been naked beneath her dress.

"This isn't just about sex, Esme. I don't want you to think that it is. It's more than that."

It was clearly visible that he was already aroused before he removed his jeans.

Equally stimulated, she watched as he pulled his tee shirt over his head.

"Well, I suppose I'd better remove these and then we are both without clothes."

Before unleashing their desires, they stood still for a moment. Feasting her eyes on his toned torso, an irresistible desire came over her. The allure of her erect nipples, signalling her arousal, drew him to her and he placed his eager mouth over hers. Without hesitation, their lips and hands explored urgently.

The magnetic attraction was intense and he

picked her up and placed her on the bed. Continuing their exploration of erogenous zones, they indulged in many tactile acts of pleasure. As a series of tremors traversed their bodies, they were finding it difficult to control their escalating surges.

He held back for a moment, not wanting to allow his own eagerness to selfishly overpower their lovemaking. Stroking the soft skin on her shoulders, he inhaled her perfume, before kissing the nape of her neck.

Unable to control her own intensifying desire for him, she arched her back provocatively as he continued to nuzzle her. Her hands explored the taut muscles in his arms and, continuing her inspection, she ran her fingers through his hairy chest. Feeling his warm breath against her skin, she relished his ongoing embraces.

Both had missed human intimacy.

She pulled him onto her. Eagerly responding to her adventurous lead, they passionately appreciated the intense closeness and immense craving for each other.

With sexual ardour mounting, they beautifully channelled their yearnings, until they both reached a mind-blowing destination of intenseness, that left them physically exhausted.

Totally satiated, they lay in each other's arms as their rapid heartbeats returned to a normal rhythm.

Holding her close, he lightly caressed her lips. It had been almost four months since his last sexual encounter. That was all it was; sex. This was different. It wasn't just about fulfilling a sexual need. It was a genuine feeling of wishing and needing to make love to her; a wonderful moment in time.

Instead of transporting them to sleep, their intimate act had been transformed into creative energy and they began chatting about the self-build project.

With artistic juices flowing, they moved into the studio area where they discussed ideas and made several sketches and notes.

Her artistic inspiration of introducing fresh concepts into his designs stimulated him. She listened before encouraging his already non-conformant ideas even further, prompting him to be more bizarre in his approach. It was as if she knew how to draw the last bit of innovative energy out of him – pushing him a bit more until he was sketching like crazy.

"Run with it, Alastair".

Raising his eyebrows, he smiled. He loved the artistic process of creating something beautiful. He loved being focused and committed.

"Some people might not get where you are coming from; but do they have to? Just listen to your intuition and then see if your clients are ok with it."

He would. Just by her being by his side, his ingenious burst of ideas were pouring out.

The only interruption to his flow was when she went downstairs to fetch two glasses of water.

"Would you like to come along with me to the appointment tomorrow?"

"I'd love to. That would be great."

Realising that it was 4.30am and his meeting with his client was scheduled for 10.30, they returned to the bedroom. Their sexual activity had not only brought them closer, it had also fuelled their inventive streaks. They'd been dynamic in more ways than one!

Like earlier on, he picked her up and carried

her to bed. Both could sense that a strong emotional bond was developing.

Before succumbing to slumber, he kissed her gently and then surprised her by showing her again how much he desired her.

"It has been said that creative souls have an insatiable passion for their work and for expressing their passion through sex."

"Well, considering what we've been up to for the last few hours, there seems to be a lot of truth in that, doesn't there? I do believe you are my muse and this is what a muse does – inspires creativeness. "

Chuckling, she cheekily retorted.

"Well, if I am to be your muse, I hope you are not expecting me to be wildly sexually adventurous and pose naked for you on a velvet chaise lounge, are you?"

"I say, yes, to both of those."

Their playful banter was mutual.

"I bet you do."

ten

She watched him as he dressed. There was something sensual about a man standing in front of a mirror fixing his tie. Leaning into him, she brushed some imaginary fluff from his lapel, straightened his already perfectly knotted tie and lightly touched his lips with her own.

His phone rang. Glancing at the name on the screen, he ignored it.

"Can I say that you look really handsome in that suit?"

Altering his posture, he thrust out his chest.

"You can."

His witty conceitedness amused her.

"Come on. Let's go. We don't want to be late."

On the journey, they talked further about the commission. This would be the second time he'd visited his clients and he was looking forward to revealing the plans; aware that they could possibly change with each visit before their final decision. He, however, was confident that they'd like his design.

"I occasionally miss the technical aspect of drawing plans. Even though I use CAD software, I still like to do rough sketches. I'm always sketching and doodling."

She'd noticed. She, also, was a doodler!

"I just love being in the thick of it all, on the sites and watching the building evolve. It's great when you see the impact it has on the owners."

When deliberating the project with him the previous evening, his intuitive energy and eclectic design expertise had impressed her. She admired how his 'fabric first' commitment to the environment would be carefully woven into the design and construction of a dwelling.

Likewise, he was equally fascinated with her knowledge of sustainable products and techniques. When perusing her designs, he'd instantly detected her extraordinary talent for appreciating spatiality and texture. She had a knack of creating a perfect balance of the feminine and masculine.

Unbeknown to him, she had intentionally researched, so that she could converse on his level.

Whilst embracing the challenge and factoring in the budget, he'd carefully considered the location and the relationship to the landscape.

The rough drawings and mood boards, which his clients had already provided on his initial visit, had enabled him to produce something spectacular.

It was fortunate that they shared the same vision as him. They'd been so excited to have been accepted onto the project. After flicking through his electronic portfolio of designs, which revealed the true extent of his breadth of self-build experience, they'd been overawed with his unique living spaces. He'd gained their trust almost immediately.

As he brought the car to a stop just outside the urban terraced house, the young couple were waiting at the door. After welcoming Alastair and Esme into the dining room, they sat around a small table and watched as the acclaimed architect proudly projected his concept onto a blank wall.

"From the information you've given me, I have created a construction which will comfortably blend in with the surrounding farm buildings and nature. I'll

61

just talk you through the intricacies of the design in stages and then you can give me your feedback."

The initial slide displayed the completed dwelling. Geometric in design, it consisted of three large boxes, connected by two tall glass atrium breezeways, which would double up as an extra lounge and a study area. The couple operated their consultancy business from home and had specified a sizable working area. The extensive use of glass and roof-lights in the breezeways would provide ample light and ventilation for this use.

"The design is flexible in that, if you wanted to add further boxes in the future, the foundations would be suitably strengthened to accommodate them."

In line with their sustainable ethos, the clients had specified that they'd like the house to have a modern industrial feel and they wanted to use some recyclable materials. He'd given them just that! The aim was to achieve a sustainable level of at least 5; level 6 being the highest.

"For the inside, I've left the oak ceiling beams uncovered, as you can see here. Against the white walls and the steel framework, I've attempted to give you the feel that you were looking for, by introducing soft lighting against the organically inspired geometric shapes."

The young couple leaned inward and beamed at each other, eager to see more of the design.

Focusing on his chiselled jawline and his strong Roman nose, Esme rested her chin on her bent wrist and attentively listened, as he artfully pitched several alternative ideas to tempt them further.

Aware of her watching him, he turned around and held her gaze, wondering whether she was aware of her sexual allure. The chemistry was palpable as they exchanged signals.

With slightly lowered eyelids, she acknowledged his look with a flutter. Casting her eyes over his broad shoulders and well-defined muscular chest, she was certain that Cupid was firing multiple erotic arrows. As her heart raced, an involuntary flushing sensation crept up her neck and onto her cheeks. To subdue the feeling, she held her palm across her throat, in an attempt to subdue the heat.

Inhaling deeply, he returned to his presentation.

"Pre-fabricated wooden sections, which would be insulated to the highest level, would be built off-site. Then, they'd be bolted into a polished concrete base, which would also have that latest underfloor heating system. To complement the aesthetics of several barn structures on the neighbouring farm, one section of the structure would have a corrugated metal roof, whilst the other two structures would be fitted with bespoke solar heating panels."

More nodding from the excited clients as they scribbled in notepads to ask questions later.

"Due to the lay of the land, the eco house will command magnificent views on all sides, especially with the expanse of glass, which would wrap around the rear and sides of the dwelling. Likewise, the breezeways and the south facing full-length windows in the boxed areas, together with the roof panels, will take great advantage of the sun's energy; thereby contributing to the sustainable ethos, which I know you want to uphold."

Pleased with their reactions, Alastair stopped for a few minutes to allow them to take further notes.

"To add interest and some colour on the

outside of the structure, in between the glass panels, a mixture of vertical and horizontal wooden larch boards would be positioned onto stainless steel invisible fixings. The environmentally-friendly timber, would be sourced from local timber merchants to be cost effective. As well as having the high-performance sustainability that you want, it would weather into an attractive silver colour and should last around sixty years or more, before it would need replacing."

He continued to explain about the living area, kitchen and bedrooms and how sustainable oak would be used in the design.

The clients smiled as he continued.

"We love it."

His designs were contemplative works of art, which were meant to provoke discussion, as this one would do. He wanted the structure to explain itself to its observers.

"Essentially, I'm contributing to the creation of modern architecture and art, by communicating my ideas and philosophies. Some people will like what I do. Others won't. I'm glad you like it."

After signing a declaration form which stated that it was his exclusive design, he downloaded the details to their email.

Sensing the energy in the room, Esme opened a small silver case and handed them a business card. She deemed it to be her identity and a more personal way of doing business.

"I'd like to offer two free consultations. I'm an interior designer and can advise on some ideas for dressing your rooms and landscaping your garden areas. My website details are on the card."

After shaking hands with the couple, Alastair

and Esme descended the steps and walked towards the car.

Focusing on her long slim legs and her high-heeled ankle straps, which clicked as she walked in front of him, he allowed his eyes to linger on her tight-fitting dress and her perfectly accentuated peach-shaped derriere.

"Do you know that I find you very sexy?"

"Do you, Alastair?"

Her nonchalance amused him and, as he opened the car door for her, he laughed heartily.

On the journey home, he continued to flirt.

"You stir something in me, Esme."

She loved the way he pronounced her name in a formal way – Es-may. She also loved his informal use of her name, Es.

As they entered the house, she pretended not to notice that he couldn't take his eyes off her.

Her perfumed body lotion lingered on her skin and, as he leant closer to her, his already-heightened testosterone levels moved up another notch. Kissing her slightly open lips, full of sexual promise, he held her tighter.

"Es. I want to show you something".

She threw him a coy sideways glance.

"Not again! What do you want to show me this time?"

eleven

He strolled through the bustling throng of shoppers in the Liverpool One area, towards the bistro where he was meeting a group of his friends and Esme. An after-work meeting had been arranged to exchange views on the homeless project.

Following their quintessential French meal, they revisited their previously discussed plan. As the project manager, Alastair had provided an update on the time constraints and achievement of milestones.

A trusted friend of his, Mr Hoffman, who was the possessor of a run-down three-storey building, had agreed to allocating one section of the property to house the homeless people for the foreseeable future.

Alastair had already drawn up plans for the renovation. Building regulations weren't required as the property had been previously used for living accommodation. Planning permission was quickly gained to add en-suites, some replacement windows and other sustainable modifications. It would be converted into seven studio apartments with the focus on sustainability and energy efficiency. There'd also be a substantial communal room, which would include a kitchen/dining area at one end and a lounge area and a gym at the opposite end. In another room, various wellbeing classes, educational/training courses and important life skills activities would be delivered. The existing roof terrace would also be renovated.

Work had commenced on the reconstruction. One group member had generously pledged the services of his construction company without charge, whilst another businessman had kindly offered to pay for all the building materials.

Another friend, who was a lawyer in the city, would donate the furniture and computer equipment for the training room.

Esme and Alastair's joint contribution would be the designing of the interiors of the building and the purchase of new modern lounge and kitchen furniture, furnishings and gym equipment. Exercise was also considered to be an important part of their rehabilitation.

Ever since he'd spoken about the project, several ideas had been milling around her head. She wanted the residents to have more than just the basic of rooms to live in. The challenge was to make the living zones feel spacious. It would be nice for them to experience some form of luxury that was dramatically different, with essential built-in storage areas in a pale wood. She was aware of the emotional power of light – both natural and artificial – and her concept would be to warm up the limited space, with quirky mood-inducing colours and different forms of lighting. She'd make it homely for them.

Each would have their own studio, which would include a lounge, kitchen area and a sleeping area with an en-suite shower room. It was her aim to greatly improve the residents' quality of life, thereby alleviating some of their problems.

As part of her work experience where she'd gathered information for her final assignment at university, she'd been involved in a renovation at a Women's Refuge, where she'd redesigned bedrooms, a lounge and a children's play area.

Unbeknown to the university, she'd disposed of the antiquated second-hand furniture and bought the soft furnishings, new bedroom furniture and carpets out of her own pocket.

Being with the women had provided her an insight into their lives, their vulnerabilities and their innermost strengths. Most of all, she'd seen how they'd do anything to protect their children. Some women did return to their husbands and she still thought about them and whether they were safe. It was their choice to return. The children had been missing the familiarity of their home and their dads.

Esme still donated a substantial allowance each month to the refuge, which helped to buy food, toiletries and clothing.

Alastair had already been in discussions with the homeless task group. Six men, who were focused on remaining dry and clean, had been identified as being suitable to live in the accommodation. They were already in recovery, attending an intensive course which promoted recovery which encouraged change and independence. Another man who wasn't substance or alcohol dependent was also identified.

Moving into the accommodation would offer inspiration and give them hope. It would also assist with restoring their confidence and increase their self-esteem.

The project group had already decided that the accommodation would be named Habitaire; which linked suitably with the Latin meaning of the word, 'to live in your own place'.

Esme initiated a discussion about the day to day running of Habitaire. The group had already decided that a caretaker/advisor position should be created and offered to a previously homeless person, thereby giving him the opportunity to attain employed status. The man had been working as a link volunteer and had gained experience of working in a homeless shelter. Another previously homeless person would cover night shifts.

Voicing her own concern for the vulnerable members of society, she addressed the group. She'd had moments of guilt when she thought about her own lifestyle and the lack of basic rights that others experienced. However, she needn't have harboured those feelings. She had always shared her monetary wealth with others. Leo had taught her that, amongst other things.

"I can't imagine how horrendous it must be for people living on the streets. The way in which they face inescapable discrimination and exclusion is so much beyond me. I don't think it's ever acceptable to accept what is humanly unacceptable."

Alastair's head tilted.

"Living within safe mid-term accommodation, which provides educational and leisure facilities, will help them to regain maximum self-reliance. If we can also help them to gain some form of employment, then it'll be easier for the men to integrate back into society."

Esme concurred.

"Why is it that we've become blind to what's staring us in the face? I've tried to imagine what it would be like to be hooked on booze or drugs, but I can't."

One of the members of the group knew first-hand what it was like to be addicted. It transpired that he'd been hiding his own issues with alcohol from his colleagues. Thankfully for him, he had not been made homeless, but he'd nearly lost his family through his drinking habit.

"We all have stuff going on in our lives. I don't need to imagine. I know. It's hard to stop drinking, especially if you have stress in your life. You just want something to take the stress away and the bottle is a temptation. I will always be an alcoholic. I know that if I just have one more drink, I'll be hooked again."

His honesty about his struggle, to resist going back to where he was before, was heart-rending and very humbling. He was now totally committed to helping others who are highly stigmatised.

He disclosed further information.

"I wondered, many times, whether my life was worth living, but I thought about my wife and kids and how they'd stuck by me. I couldn't do it! I couldn't put them through any more pain. Something clicked within my head. It gave me a jolt. If I can improve the lives of others, I'll do my very best to make a difference."

Impressed with his honesty, Esme discerned that human behaviour is complex. Some people deal with suffering better than others. She was also aware of how we all experience dark and light within our lives. It's about recognising the difference between the two.

After approving deadlines and the completion date, the meeting ended.

Flirting with each other, they strolled arm in arm through the city centre.

"I want to show you something when we get home."

Her sensuous smile was enticing. She rolled her eyes as she visualised their unclothed bodies joining together.

"I wonder what that might be!"

twelve

Whilst eating breakfast, his phone rang. Glancing at the screen, he cut the call. A text followed, which he ignored, followed by yet another call, which he cut off again.

She noticed that he seemed agitated as a further text followed.

He glanced over at her and knew she would be wondering why he was cutting the calls.

"Sorry, Es. I know it's rude of me, to have my phone in close proximity whilst we're eating. I'm trying to break the habit. It's something I've been working on."

Fortunately for him, the dating agency rang, asking if he wanted to renew his subscription.

"No, that won't be necessary. You did a great job. The match was perfect."

Intrigued, she watched as he smiled, pointed towards her and raised his thumb.

Returning to his conversation, she discerned it was the agency he was speaking to.

"Thank you for all your help."

He walked over to her and held her close to him. Yes. The coordinating of their details had been accurate.

"Do you know who that was, Es?"

Before she had time to answer, her phone rang.

"Hello Esme. Just a polite catch up. Having just spoken with Alastair, am I correct in presuming that you also want to cancel your subscription?"

"Hello. Yes, you would be correct."

thirteen

He watched her as she sang a medley of songs in the shower. Unable to resist, he stripped off and joined her.

After allowing the water to cascade down their bodies, he reached over and turned off the dial.

Grabbing the bath sheet, he draped it around her before carrying her over to the bed.

"I want to show you something, Es."

"I bet you do, Alastair. You do know that we're expected to meet the others in half an hour?"

"This won't take long."

****

Knowing something special was occurring and engulfed in the first throes of love, they walked hand in hand over to Number One, where Stefano and Camellia had already welcomed the other guests.

As they walked up the path, the door opened to greet them.

"Hi Esme. Nice to see you, Alastair. I thought it was you. I saw you the other day as you drove in. How are you doing?

"I'm good thanks. You?"

Smiling, Stefano nodded. His guest had been a frequent visitor to his restaurants, but he hadn't seen him of late.

As he was introduced to the other neighbours, his eyes scanned the space, which had been designed over three floors. A massive artistic element, in the form of a large sculptural piece of lighting, hung from the top floor ceiling into the well of a dramatic marble staircase.

Following polite conversation with Trish and Nick and Dave and Tina, Stefano showed him around the ground floor. Two en-suite bedrooms and an open-plan lounge leading onto a kitchen/dining area, with an enclosed utility room to the rear, slotted comfortably into the sizeable area.

In the massive seamless space on the first level, was the main lounge area, a further capacious professional kitchen and a large dining table which could easily seat twelve people.

Situated on the second floor, were two further en-suite bedrooms, with views which overlooked the sprawling countryside.

He particularly liked the lack of ornamentation and functionality throughout the house. Structural plants had been cleverly placed to, not only add colour and enhance the overall appearance of the space, but to create a healthier environment by eliminating air pollutants.

During conversation, as presumed, he learnt that all four houses in Chancel Quarter carried an aesthetic continuity, containing the latest built-in technology.

However, the layout and functionality of each dwelling was unique.

After dinner, he was given a tour of the other two houses and observed that block colours had been sparingly used, with just a splash of primary tints and hues of black, tans, greys and whites.

Together with excellent use of ambient and

accent lighting, occasional structured plants had also been used as a feature in those houses.

Not unlike many of the dwellings he had designed, he was impressed with how the architect had allowed the natural light to flow through the spaces, by introducing floor-to-ceiling windows.

He was further impressed with the way the he had incorporated the 'fabric first approach' into his minimalist and sustainable 'green credential' designs. All of the houses were carbon neutral and high rated.

Even though the residents jointly employed a gardener to undertake the heavy work, the three men had admitted to being fanatical about keeping their grounds tidy and, most weekends, they could be seen pottering amongst the plants and hedges.

From the way questions were being fired at him, Alistair discerned that he was being closely vetted by Esme's protective neighbours. He supposed it was only natural that they'd want to know more about his background.

After returning to Stefano ad Camellia's house, they all resumed their previous positions around the dining table and nibbled at more delicacies.

Alastair broached the subject of the piece of land at the side of Stefano and Camellia's house.

"Have you ever thought of building on that piece of land, Stefano?"

Camellia glanced at the others around the table, as her husband waited before answering. They were a highly territorial group and didn't want anyone else invading their sanctuary.

"It has been discussed previously, but we're not interested in having another construction on this development. We are content with the balance of the four houses. An additional would make it look too crammed."

Silence ensued, as the others nodded.

Sensing a synergetic loyalty within the group, he changed tack.

"I do agree. This setting is spectacular. Another dwelling would certainly disturb the balance. It's just my entrepreneurial head working overtime!"

Esme quickly diverted the conversation to the renovation of the run-down chantry at the rear of their properties.

"Why don't we see if we can do something with it. We could tidy it up."

Stefano smiled at her appropriate interjection.

"Great idea. I'll approach the owners of the chantry ruins and see if they're agreeable to us tidying the area. They still own that piece of land."

Esme rerouted the conversation again.

"Tell them about the homeless proposition, Alastair."

As he communicated his plan, they all listened intently and were interested in becoming involved.

Trish and Nick agreed to provide and instal double glazing units to the cracked and rotted window frames. Dave and Tina would pledge a generous supply of bedding, towels and sundry items for each apartment. Stefano and Camellia would guarantee a weekly supply of foodstuffs, essential toiletries and cleaning items.

Sitting opposite Alastair, Esme slipped off her shoe and discreetly teased the space at the top of his socks with her bare foot.

Pleasantly distracted, his eyes widened as the corners of his mouth raised slightly.

Hypnotised by the way he was staring at her, she clumsily misjudged her mouth and almost spilled her wine as she raised the glass to her lips.

Amused, he observed her glistening pupils dilate as she returned his gaze, before looking away. She was so utterly irresistible!

He pondered on whether the rest of the group had picked up on their chemistry. Even though he was trying to be subtle, it was blatantly obvious to the group that he was devouring her with his twinkling blue eyes.

Tilting her head to one side, she exposed more of her bare shoulder, whilst caressing the rim of her wine glass. Attentive and approving of his every word, her apparent endearment was obvious.

Throwing her another flirty sideways glance, he winked.

Being very much in tune with her own sexual energy, she knew exactly what she was doing. With lips parted, she rested her forefinger on her bottom lip and fluttered her naturally long eyelashes before turning away from him. Resuming her conversation with Stefano, she tried to appear calm.

His prolonged eye contact had caused her heart to skip a few beats and she blushed. Whenever he'd held her gaze before, intimacy always occurred afterwards.

With raised eyebrows and knowing grins, their captive audience had been suitably entertained as they furtively watched the unspoken passion and uncontrollable pull between Alastair and Esme in the blissful first throes of love .

fourteen

At breakfast, the following morning, his phone rang. He decided to answer it this time.

"I need to speak to you."

"It's not convenient. I'll call you within the hour."

He'd have to deal with it sooner or later and it had to be sooner! The texts and phone calls had to stop.

"Everything ok?"

He nodded; his furrowed brow and pursed lips indicating otherwise.

Esme's innate ability to read his edginess, surprised her, as he visibly struggled to get his words out.

"I just need to... just need to go somewhere."

"Ok."

She didn't probe. Obviously, it was important.

She busied herself whilst he went out into the garden, phone in hand, returning a few minutes later.

"Es, I need to go out. I shouldn't be too long."

"Is everything alright, Alastair."

Flustered, he nodded.

"Yes. It will be. I've just got to sort something."

Instantly absorbing his sudden frustration, she inwardly questioned his strangely secretive behaviour.

Trying not to be overly concerned, she continued to load the dishwasher.

Before leaving, he held her forearm, leant over and kissed her.

"Won't be too long. See you later."

fifteen

Sitting by the window in a café just further down from Hoopers, she stared out, watching the rain bucketing it down onto the road. It was unbelievable. Only a few minutes before, the sun had been shining.

Then she saw him, running across the road with his coat thrown over his head, to stop him getting drenched. Her heart did a somersault. He was still as handsome and as stylish as ever.

Shaking his coat in the entrance, he opened the door and looked around for her.

"Over here, Alastair."

He walked over to her and sat down.

"What's the matter, Jen? Why do you keep on ringing me?"

"Oh! No hello, then. Aren't you going to ask me how I am?"

"Why do you need to speak to me. I thought we'd said all what we had to say after the divorce."

The waitress came and asked for their order.

"Just an orange juice for me, please."

"May I have another Americano, please?"

Whilst still smartly dressed, he noticed that she'd let herself go somewhat. Her hair wasn't as neat as it usually was and there were dark circles under her eyes.

"Why are you so hostile with me, Alastair?"

"I just want to know why you keep ringing me."

She bowed her head and took a sip of her half-filled cup of coffee, which was now cold.

"I've really missed you. Will you come home?"

With mouth agape and open palms raised, he couldn't believe what he was hearing. He wondered how he'd ever swallowed her lies.

"What are you saying, Jen? NO! You are nicely settled in the house which I built for us both. You took me to the cleaners, didn't you? You got more than half of what you deserved."

"I'm sorry."

"What's the matter. Has he traded you in for a younger model?"

She didn't answer. His harsh words had cut deep. Her younger lover had done just that.

"I just lost my way, Alastair. I only realised how much I loved you after the divorce. I only appreciated what I had when it was too late."

Fiddling with his keys on the table, he was having none of her excuses.

"You hurt me. You played with my mind. The abject humiliation I suffered in work after I found out about you cheating on me. The irony was that I wasn't the first to know. Someone from my office saw you in a night club in Manchester with him. You were all over him. They didn't say anything until afterwards. They felt sorry for me. How do you think that made me feel?"

Again, she bowed her head, as the waitress brought their drinks.

"Will you just think about it? I don't mind waiting for your answer."

Shaking his head in disbelief, he tried to refrain from raising his voice.

"What the hell are you talking about here? You

were having sex with another man in our bed, in our house and you want me to come back to live with you. I can't believe I'm hearing this."

"What did you expect me to do, whilst you were working away in different countries? Just sit in and wait for you to come home. You were always working, or having meetings, or visiting clients. We didn't have much time together. I was lonely. It just happened."

He'd give her that. He was always away. She had a point.

"On reflection, I will admit that I put my work first, but everything I did, I did for us, so that we would have a bloody good standard of living. I didn't have a clue that you weren't happy. You were a damn good actress."

"Please, Alastair. Please forgive me. Will you reconsider coming home?"

Her cheap words and meaningless chatter fell on deaf ears.

"There is nothing to consider! There is no second chance! I've moved on from you. What don't you understand about the word NO?"

Between her sobs, she managed to speak.

"I heard you're with someone else now. Is that true?"

The damned cheek of her. What the fucking hell did it have to do with her, who he was with? Had she been stalking him?

"Yes. You heard right. It's true."

Still crying, she wouldn't give up.

"What's she like? Where did you meet her?"

"It doesn't matter what she's like. I'm going now."

"Don't go. Don't leave me whilst I'm feeling this way."

"Bye. You left me, remember?"

She reached out for his hand and moved towards him.

"What I did was wrong and I'm sorry. Can you forgive me?"

"Yes. I can forgive you, but don't ring me again. I won't answer your call."

He left a twenty-pound note on the table for the drinks and, without looking at her, he walked out of the café.

On his way back to the car, he noticed that the rain had stopped. The sun had come out. He thought about the absurd encounter and how her grovelling apologies sickened him. Did she really think he'd take her back?

Totally unaware that his karmic relationship with Jen wasn't meant to last, it was only meant for him to learn, he was glad he'd agreed to meet her, if only for closure.

His life was with Esme now.

sixteen

Whilst waiting for him to return, she'd been busy working on her latest commission. Work was the wrong definition; she was shuffling fabric and colour swatches around, trying to make some sense of what was going on. Her mind was working overtime. He'd been gone for a couple of hours.

She'd already rustled up two large helpings of lemon syllabub and was preparing some herbed salmon for dinner, when the front door opened. Momentarily, she'd forgotten that he had the code to the external gate and she had given him a door key. His appearance had startled her.

Turning towards him, she smiled as he took her in his arms and held her close.

"What's wrong, Alastair?"

"I'll pour us some wine and then I'll tell you."

Sitting opposite each other at the kitchen island, he relayed what had happened.

"Is that why you kept cutting off those calls?"

"Yes."

"Can I ask you something?"

He nodded.

"Why did you keep her number in your phone? Why didn't you just delete it?"

He shrugged. A significant silence ensued.

"I don't know. I just did."

Taking another gulp of her wine, she felt a little hurt that he hadn't initially been straight with her about the phone call.

"It just seems strange that you didn't tell me. Did you think I would mind?"

"I don't know what I thought, Es. Maybe, I just wanted some sort of closure; to tell her what I really thought of what she did to me."

"I wouldn't have minded if you'd told me. Your furtive behaviour was making me a little suspicious. Did you get closure?"

Seeing the sadness in her face, he felt disloyal for not telling her in the first place. Why had he kept her number in his phone? Picking up his phone, she watched as he deleted Jen's number.

"Yes. I did. In fact, on the way home, I realised just how much I love you. I'm sorry if I made you anxious. I didn't mean to."

Had she heard correctly? He'd just said he loved her! Her stomach muscles tightened. She felt dizzy.

"I'm not a jealous person, Alastair. Just be honest with me in future. Trust is everything."

She leant back in her chair and looked him in the eye, thinking of how she'd feel if he wasn't in her life. It wouldn't be her choice!

"I just didn't think. I won't hurt you, Es. I love you."

He'd said it again! Knowing their connection was solid enough to put this pointless episode behind them, she discerned it would be immature to prolong something that had happened before she'd met him.

"Undoubtedly, you were right to want closure. I can understand that. Let's forget it and move on. It was in the past. I don't even know her."

As he gazed into her eyes, he suddenly felt

very protective towards her. He wouldn't hurt her. He knew what it felt like!

"Pour some more of that wine. Let's celebrate the closing of that chapter in your life."

seventeen

Several evenings later, all the residents of Chancel Quarter were sat in Camellia and Stefano's lounge, listening to them reveal the generations who had lived in the White House and those descendants, who had been laid to rest within the ancient chantry.

Sipping their gin and tonics and Peroni's, they watched an informative presentation, which had been projected onto the lounge wall.

Camellia, with permission from the previous owners of the White House, had enjoyed transferring numerous images of the inside of the dwelling and its occupants into the Powerpoint document; all of which revealed how life had been lived in previous centuries.

The house and the chantry had been two magnificent pieces of architecture. With the passage of time, the chantry and the gravestones, which had previously been kept in a reasonable state of repair, were now reduced to a ruin and some weather-worn rubble. Only the foundations, a stone altar and three walls of irregular heights remained. The other parts had been destroyed in a bombing raid.

Admiring its features, Alastair could see that it had been built in a baroque style. There had been a stone staircase leading up to an arched doorway which had two ornate pillars at the side of it.

They learnt that the owners were a devoted Catholic family. The local priest would go there to say masses for the repose of the souls of deceased and say prayers for surviving members.

They were further informed that the chantry had been dedicated to Our Lady of Mount Carmel. The sister of the lady who owned the house, had devoted her life to God and had entered the Carmelite Order and on 16th July each year, a Mass had been celebrated to honour the feast day and in remembrance of their relative.

An image of the nun in a brown scapular was then beamed onto the wall and a faded picture of one of the chantry windows, which had a glass-stained window depicting Mary, the Mother of God, followed.

Another faded image was of a statue of Mary holding Jesus, after he'd been crucified on the cross. It was adorned with the initials 'INRI'.

Camellia had explained that this was the Latin notice which Pontius Pilate had nailed over Jesus' head, as he lay dying on the cross.. Translated into English, it means 'Jesus of Nazareth, King of the Jews'.

Although some of the neighbours weren't Catholics, they still found the history fascinating.

She also revealed that the family had donated substantial amounts of funding to the Carmelite training colleges around England and the poor people in the parish.

Whilst she'd been sifting through the endless family records, Camellia had found a prayer and she handed a copy to each of them as a keepsake.

> **Prayer to**
> **Our Lady of Mount Carmel**
> **Feast Day: July 16th**
>
> Most beautiful flower of Mount Camel, Fruitful Vine, Splendour of Heaven, Mother of the Son of God and Immaculate Virgin, assist me in my hour of need. Star of the Sea, help me and show me that you are my Mother.
>
> Holy Mary, Mother of God, Queen of Heaven and Earth, I humbly ask you from the bottom of my heart, to assist me in my hour of need. There are none that can withstand your power.
>
> Show me that you are my Mother. Mary, conceived without sin, pray for us who have recourse to you. (3 times)
>
> Dear Mother, I place this cause in your hands. (3 times)

Coincidentally, Camellia proceeded to inform her audience that 16th July was also her birthday.

"I'd like to sing something for you. I used to sing in the choir when I lived in Italy."

As she sang 'Ave Maria' in Latin, the group were in awe of her impromptu soprano rendition.

Following her performance, Stefano spoke of how the family who owned the weather-worn ruins, had welcomed the idea of renovating the graveyard and had happily given their permission, to undertake restoration work.

It was agreed that the group would undertake the clearing process on the following Sunday.

eighteen

From a keen photographer's perspective, the ancient overgrown graveyard was a perfect place to take some shots of a piece of ancient history. Esme walked around the remains and clicked her camera. The images would be included in an album, which would be presented to the owners of the graveyard and the chantry .

The unkempt land, with its overgrown trees and wildflowers growing organically between the leaning gravestones, was a perfect backdrop for the sacred place.

Inside the chantry, Alastair had unearthed numerous large stone boulders which had been hidden under the mounds of lichen, moss and other debris. With small beads of sweat trickling down his forehead and wet patches on his shirt, he crouched down and carefully gathered each piece, before siting them outside the remains of the crumbling stonework, in readiness for them being returned to their original position within the structure of the building.

Little did he know, that in the not-too-distant future, he would find much-needed solace by sitting within this tranquil place.

Intrigued with his finds, he began to figure out where the dislodged pieces would fit. Inside the rear of the chantry, beneath some trailing overgrown moss, he'd also discovered the faint outline of the Carmelite symbol engraved on one of the walls.

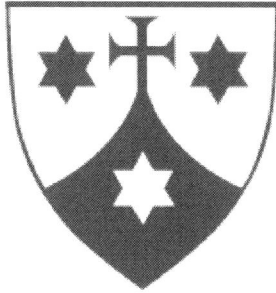

Far from being eerie, it was a peaceful place. The positive camaraderie and teamwork was evident, as the graveyard succumbed to the gentle hands of its visiting strangers, allowing them to repair its decaying existence.

Whilst the other men were busy straightening the faded gravestones, wedging them up until they could cement them in securely, the women were digging up the plants and placing them in several buckets of water. They'd be replanted in different areas, after the sacred place had been cleared and the gravestones cleaned.

When a gentle breeze suddenly appeared, to cool them from the rays of the midday sun, Esme took it as a sign that the chantry was thanking them all for their efforts.

She recalled how she'd go for walks with her mother in the local cemetery when she was a little girl. Her friends had questioned why she would want to go to a place where dead people were buried.

Once most of the strenuous work had been completed, amidst clouds of dust and shovelled dirt, they all rested their tired bodies on the new benches that had been conveniently delivered the day before; Temporarily placed underneath some ancient oak trees, until they could even the rough ground and be laid onconcrete base. The workers welcomed the shade as they sat there, tucking into their lunch.

Alastair made a list of what materials would need to be delivered before next week, to complete the heavy work. All of the men would work together to replace the fallen stonework.

Trish and Nick had already commissioned a stained-glass window of Our Lady, exactly like the one in the photograph that Camellia had shown them. The artist had promised to have it ready for the following week, at a hefty price!

By the end of the day, the remains of the chantry looked much neater, as did the surrounding area. The cleansed gravestones, which proudly bore the weathered and faded names of family generations, evoked an emotive piece of history.

Esme had kindly offered to re-letter the barely visible names with gold stone paint.

nineteen

The following Sunday saw the residents, suitably kitted out again to continue the renovation. Spades, rakes numerous garden tools and building materials were placed neatly in piles, ready to be used. Several cool boxes had been filled with food and drinks, to sustain them throughout the hot day.

Cleverly mixing the man-made products and reusing the ancient stones which had been buried under the overgrown mossy grass, the busy residents reverentially tended the land.

More of the overgrown grass had been cut and several dead branches on the overhanging trees had been sensitively pruned. New flowers and bulbs were planted alongside the existing sweet-scented plants, ingeniously transforming the shady area.

Using the ancient flagstones, the men worked tirelessly, laying a path which led up to the chantry.

Trish and Nick deftly manoeuvred the replica stained-glass window inside the newly repointed sandstone arch. The shades of blue and gold glistened as the sun forced its way through the trees to highlight its splendour.

Alastair and Stefano returned to securing the heavy gravestones with a mixture of sand and cement.

During the previous week, Esme had laboured for three days restoring the names with gold paint and her handiwork was impressive.

As they tried to manoeuvre a weighty piece of marble, a sudden gust of wind encircled them.

Remaining still, they stared in unsettled awe, as a silvery mist silently encompassed the area around the chantry, absorbing the goings on before eerily drifting off into the ether.

Esme whispered in their direction.

"We're sorry for disturbing you. We're only here to make your resting ground tidy. We respect you."

The others glanced warily towards each other, wondering if Esme often spoke to spirits.

Alastair had heard her talking to herself on several occasions, but he didn't think anything of it. He'd done the same when he'd been running through ideas in his head.

Observing their reactions, she deftly deflected their attention.

"Let's eat, shall we?"

Over lunch, they spoke of how they'd like to commemorate the Feast Day of Our Lady of Mount Carmel each year, as a respectful way of preserving the memories of past generations.

They also discussed ideas of how they'd reveal the transformation of the chantry to the remaining family members of the descendants.

Later in the afternoon, after much more work had been completed, Camellia jokingly voiced her appreciation to the others.

"Hey, what a great team we make! Besides it being a serene space for silent reflection, it will also give the men yet another place to potter around.

Stefano guffawed, but he wasn't complaining.

"Thanks, Cam. That's just another thing to add to my already elongated list of jobs to do!"

twenty

Within minutes of leaving the busy motorway, the roads became quieter as they carefully navigated their way down several narrow country lanes, with only enough space for a single vehicle.

"I'm so relieved that we've finally reached the countryside. There's some very crazy drivers out there today."

She nodded.

"It's to be expected, isn't it? It *is* Friday. They'll all be rushing home for the weekend."

On either side of them, the high stone-built walls were an indication that they were nearing the quaint village of Silverdale, a small community located within the border of Lancashire.

Although he'd visited many places in England, he hadn't been to this area before.

"It didn't take us long, did it?"

"No. Depending on the traffic, I usually do it in an hour and a half."

Having skirted the village, they caught their first glimpse of the coast. As the constricted country lane in front of them started to ascend, to the left they could see the beauty of the bay that lay below.

Alastair was amazed at the spectacular view.

"Wow. I wasn't expecting that."

After a sudden sharp right turn, the whole of the bay became visible through the rear-view mirror and they were distracted from the view by a sign informing them, that they were now entering the county of Cumbria.

Observing his reactions, she smiled as they passed a charming dwelling, known as Priory Cottage. She knew the people who owned it; having spoken to them on many occasions during her daily strolls when she stayed at her holiday lodge.

"That house looks as if it's an illustration from a children's fairy tale book."

"Yes. It does. Inside is just as quaint. They've managed to retain the cottage style throughout."

As he slowly manoeuvred their car along the lane, another cottage came into view. A tiny front gate and a picket fence surrounded the whole of the plot perimeter. A cacophony of colours welcomed visitors to the area. Foxgloves, geraniums, hollyhocks and lupins all lived harmoniously together within the front garden. Honeysuckle was growing freely along the fence and pink rose bushes stood at either side of the path which led up to the front door. It was so typical of an English country garden which was pictured on the front of a chocolate box from the 1960's.

A small red rectangular post box, set within a stone wall, signalled the entrance to an even narrower side lane which led them into the tiny hamlet of Far Arnside.

He drove slowly, but If they had encountered another vehicle coming the other way, one of them would have had to reverse. Fortunately, the road was clear of oncoming traffic and, as they neared the end of the lane, the lodge came into view.

"We're nearly there now. It's a dead end, so we'll be ok from here on."

On the final downward approach, the view was breathtaking. The roof of the lodge, which was perched comfortably on a rocky outcrop, overlooking the largest estuary in northwest England, appeared to be parallel to the horizon.

Esme had bought the lodge after Leo had died. It had afforded her some sanctuary in her time of grieving.

Stepping out of the car, he walked towards the edge and peered over. The gentle lapping of the waves were already soothing him. The remote location gave an overwhelming sense of calm. The only sounds were of the birds tweeting and the delicate trickling sound of water, which came from a channel leading to the sea; coming to rest in the shingle bay just a few meters below the deck.

Surveying the outside of the lodge and its position, he was particularly impressed with the design. A wrap-around decked terrace made it possible to take in every aspect of the magnificent scenic coastline and the surrounding countryside.

"Hey, Es. This is something special, isn't it?"

Collecting their bags from the car, he followed her inside.

Walking from room to room, he was equally impressed. The generous lounge area, with its full-width windows, overlooked the vast expanse of seacoast. At one end was a modern kitchen and down a corridor were two ample-sized bedrooms and a shower room.

Being in an elevated position, he discerned that the lodge had been designed with large picture windows to take in the magnificent view of the bay, which straddled two counties. As he looked to the other side, he could see cattle grazing in a sloping field and a calming sense of peace enveloped him.

Following their evening meal, they sat on the terrace enjoying the stillness and calm of the moment.

As daylight started to fade, the sun suddenly dipped below a large cloud, revealing a blazing orange ball of light which cast a vivid, blinding reflection across the sea towards them.

Drinking champagne, they toasted each other and quietly reflected on the sheer splendour of the spectacular nature which encompassed them.

twenty one

The following morning, as the sun cast direct beams of light through the double doors at the side of the lounge, they ate breakfast outside on the terrace, watching the lapping waves making their way towards them.

"Shall we take a morning stroll, Es? You can show me around the area."

"Yes. Of course. There's so many picturesque walks around here."

After changing into some suitable walking gear, they made their way along the beach and rocky coastal path to the delightful seaside village of Arnside.

Whilst passing a short parade of local shops along the promenade, Alastair stopped to peer in the window of a local bakery and was enticed by the artisan breads and pastries displayed in baskets in the window.

Armed with freshly-baked bread and two lemon tarts, they passed a fish and chip shop which overlooked the estuary.

As he perused the menu, Esme informed him that it was the best fish and chip shop for miles around.

"We'll come here one evening and have some supper. You'll love it. I've been here many times."

Deciding to take an alternative route back, they veered off the coastal path and followed a rather steep trail through an area of woodland which led to Arnside Knott. From the breezy hilltop summit, they admired the stunning views over the Kent Valley and Lakeland Fells. Such was the magnificent view from the top of the Knott, it was more than worth the effort to climb to the peak and take in the incredible vistas in every direction.

By the time they'd reached home, they were pleasantly tired and decided to retire to the bedroom for an afternoon siesta.

After showering together, they lay on the bed, relaxing and chatting idly.

Esme drifted off and, taking the opportunity to prepare the evening meal, he crept out of bed and tiptoed into the kitchen.

****

Later that evening, they sat outside again on the terrace. Alastair had produced a gourmet dinner of crab stuffed mushrooms on a bed of rocket drizzled with fig balsamic vinegar, pan-seared salmon with a herbed crust and asparagus dipped in lemon and herb butter. The Sicilian lemon tarts, which he'd bought earlier, were served with a quenelle of rhubarb ice cream.

As he cleared the table, she leant over the balustrade, breathing in the magnificent scenery and enjoying the balmy caresses of the light wind on her face. Tingles of excitement filled her stomach.

He returned with a bottle of Bollinger la Grande Annee 2008 Vintage champagne in a silver ice bucket and two cut-glass flutes on a tray, which he'd sneakily stored in the boot of his car before leaving home.

She raised her eyebrows and smiled.

"This drinking of champagne is becoming a habit."

He popped the cork and carefully tipped the flute as he poured the full-bodied, ice-cold, sparkling liquid into it, before handing it to her. Filling his own flute, he sat beside her.

"Close your eyes, Es."

As he placed a white leather-bound box into the palms of her hands, she allowed her fingers to trace around the size of the square case.

"Now open them."

Holding the box in both hands, she paused for a moment.

"Are you going to open it?"

Gazing into his eyes, she nodded.

Inside, resting on a bed of red velvet, was a ring. A triangle-cut three carat white diamond with perfectly pointed corners, dazzled brilliantly on a narrow platinum band. Touching the concentric rows of parallel facets, which resembled a rising staircase, she trembled.

He looked at her and waited for a reaction. Even though Jen's rejection had left him scarred and scared to love again, he knew what he felt for Es was powerful. It had only been just over seven weeks since he'd first met her in person, but he was open to taking a chance on love again.

She was shocked. It was unexpected. Pressing her right outstretched palm tightly across her breasts, she attempted to suppress her rapid heartbeats.

"Will you marry me, Es? I know it's only been a short time since we've known each other, but I feel as if I've known you forever."

Shaking, her vision was blurred as she gazed into his eyes. Still wearing Leo's rings on her left hand, she touched each ring and held them tightly.

Trembling, as he waited for her answer. There were only so many tomorrows and he wanted to be her husband; if she'd have him.

She could hear Leo's voice, whispering in her subconscious, encouraging her to accept his offer of marriage.

"Yes. I will, Alastair."

Taking Leo's rings from her left hand, she placed them on her right ring finger. She'd always wear them.

He took the ring and carefully slid it onto her left ring finger.

"You've just made me one happy man, Esme Clarke."

Taking her hands, he pulled her towards him and pecked her lips gently several times, then more passionately.

Toasting their engagement, they leant over the balustrade drinking the golden-hued champagne and watching the sun set beyond the horizon.

They'd seal their engagement in a different way, later.

twenty two

On return from their stay at the lodge, he'd put his house up for sale. She'd also given notice to her tenants, who were living in the three properties she owned. Fortunately, their tenancies were due to be renewed and so the timing was right. Even luckier, all of the tenants wanted to buy the homes they'd been living in.

By the end of the following week, he'd also sold his house to the first viewer.

An appointment with the register office had also been arranged, where the necessary paperwork had been produced for inspection and completed, so that a date could be arranged.

They'd visited their neighbours individually, to inform them of their engagement and wedding plans.

Even though some of them may have thought it was a bit soon for them to get married, they politely didn't voice their views. It was obvious that Esme and Alastair were compatible and, anyhow, life was about taking chances!

In the months preceding the wedding, they visited the design studio where Alastair had purchased Esme's engagement ring. Deciding on identical rings, the jeweller had promised to have them ready, in time for their wedding which would take place in two months' time.

They'd decided to hold the reception in their own home and, after several meetings with Stefano and Camellia about catering arrangements, the food and drinks had also been sorted.

It was to be a small, intimate wedding and their neighbours were the only ones to be invited. Esme had already distanced herself from the Cheshire Set and so none of those acquaintances, or Alastair's colleagues, had been given an invite.

It was to be a totally private affair.

twenty three

They'd already been awake several hours, watching the sunrise, when they heard a loud knocking on the door.

As Alastair opened the door, he was greeted by Stefano and Camellia.

Stefano lifted a silver hostess trolley over the threshold and wheeled it into the kitchen area.

Camellia then presented him with a bottle of Louis Roeder Cristal Rose 2004 champagne, immersed in a bucket of ice.

As he welcomed them in, Esme floated down the stairs in a silky white dressing gown.

Her face beaming, she hugged them both.

"Well, what a wonderful surprise. Thank you."

Camellia noticed how glowing she looked. Being in love had the power to make you look that way.

"Just a little wedding breakfast for you both. You'll need something to keep you going until later. Enjoy."

Alastair retrieved the champagne flutes from one of the cabinets and placed them on the kitchen island, whist Esme excitedly opened the trolley doors.

Inside were two platters, artistically arranged with slices of smoked salmon, avocado and steamed asparagus.

On another plate were thick chunks of cheesy soda bread and a small dish filled with butter curls.

Tiny freshly-made cinnamon pancakes were

heaped onto another plate, accompanied with a dish of Greek yoghurt and jug of rhubarb coulis.

He twisted the bottle and removed the cork.

Holding the flute at an angle, he slowly poured the fizzing salmon-pink liquid down the side of the tall-stemmed crystal glass until it was half-full. Examining the ice-cold bubbles as they danced around the side, he nodded as he handed it to her.

Using the same procedure, he poured another glass for himself and inhaled the aromatic scents of strawberry and orange, before returning the gold-coloured bottle into the bucket of ice.

Lifting their flutes, they toasted each other.

"To us Esme and our future."

"To us Alastair. I'm so thankful that we met."

As she sipped the crispy citrus champagne, the initial mouthful quickly entered her bloodstream and she embraced the light-headed sensation that it gave her. With the aftertaste lingering on her taste buds, she took another sip; remembering other exhilarating occasions when they'd drank similar champagnes.

"Do you know something? I can remember reading an article about how scientists had revealed that moderate consumption of champagne improved the memory and, the antioxidants in it were also good for the heart and the skin."

"Well, we'd better begin drinking more of it then. What say you?"

She smiled at him and nodded.

"I'd better eat. I feel a bit tipsy."

Amidst their combination of excitement and nervous energy, they hungrily tucked into the delicious breakfast feast, chatting animatedly about the day ahead of them and their future together.

After pouring the remainder of the sparkling champagne, he handed her a white leather box.

Transfixed, he couldn't take his eyes off her.

Opening the narrow case, she glanced at him and wiped away her tears of happiness with her linen napkin. Inside, on a bed of white velvet, lay a thin platinum bracelet inset with the same diamonds that were in her engagement ring and their wedding rings.

Placing the bracelet around her slender wrist and securing the fastener, his bottom lip quivered and his eyes were moist.

She leant over and kissed him.

"Thank you, darling. It's beautiful. I love it."

"I thought you might. I asked him to create it especially for you when we went to buy the rings."

Quickly remembering the gift she'd bought for him, she ran upstairs.

"Won't be a minute."

A few moments later, she returned with a large white envelope and handed it to him.

He flipped through the information in the envelope, which contained visual images of a tastefully decorated villa in the village of Frigliana.

"What's this? You haven't bought this villa for me, have you?"

Not expecting his swift reaction, she shook her head and chuckled.

"No. I haven't."

"What is it then?"

"I know that we said that we'd delay our honeymoon and that we'd go to the lodge for a few days, but I've been longing to visit this beautiful little village in Spain again. It's only about 45 kms from Malaga and I thought we could just go there later, after we've completed our commissions."

He threw back his head and laughed loudly.

"That was a surprise! I thought you'd bought it!"

"Well, I couldn't think of anything to buy for the man who has everything, so I thought I'd book the villa for our honeymoon."

"I do have everything. I have you!"

****

As she walked out of her dressing room, dressed in a slinky off-the-shoulder creation which skimmed the contours of her slender frame, Alastair's heart missed a beat as she approached him.

"Oh! Es! You look stunning."

Admiring her irresistible husband-to-be, in his impeccably tailored light grey suit, she went weak at the knees.

Enclosed in a fine mist of the Creed Neroli Sauvage perfume that they both shared, he leaned in and gently brushed her lips with his.

"You look very handsome in that suit, darling. Italian?"

Raising his eyebrows, he smiled.

She gently wiped the smear of pink lipstick from his lips and thought how lucky she was to have met him.

Picking up her simple bouquet, she clutched the trailing gypsy grass flowers in front of her and her mind returned to the last time she'd held a wedding bouquet.

Holding her breath, she just knew that Leo would approve of her marrying Alastair.

She thought she could hear his Irish dulcet

tones. Expecting him to be there, she turned around and felt his presence.

"You look so beautiful, Esme. You deserve some happiness. You shouldn't be alone."

A tear escaped and she wiped it away with the back of her forefinger.

As Alastair opened the front door, there was a round of applause from their neighbours.

On reaching the register office, the celebrant welcomed them, before ushering them into a side room to reiterate the order of service .

Alastair entered the room first and took his place at the front.

As the music announced the entrance of the bride, the rapid clicking sounds of Dave's camera could also be heard as he captured memories of their special day.

Esme linked Stefano's arm as they walked slowly down the aisle to the sound of Van Morrison's, 'Have I Told You Lately That I Love you?'

When they reached the end of the aisle, he positioned her at the side of her husband-to-be and sat on the seat next to Camellia.

The ceremony was brief, lasting a mere fifteen minutes. Even though vows weren't required in the register office, the bride and groom expressed their own emotional words of commitment before placing their platinum and diamond wedding bands on each other's ring fingers.

On their return to Chancel Quarter, they were surprised to be applauded by Stefano's head chef and his assistants, as they entered their home.

The clapping continued as the others followed them.

Presented with flutes of the same champagne that they'd drank earlier, their guests raised a toast to the newly-weds and ate a selection of cheddar and leak tartlets, mozzarella and sun-dried tomato canapes and smoked trout and potato blinis, before sitting down to a spectacular feast.

Taking centre place on the formally laid out table with eight place settings, stood a spectacular wedding cake resembling the shape of Esme and Alastair's house.

Stefano's professionalism was in the design and decoration of custom-made cakes. He'd spent most of the previous evening completing the white blocked creation.

Whilst the head chef discreetly lingered in the background, overseeing the flawless service of the four courses, two female waiters served an elegantly stacked starter, consisting of three perfectly formed circles of tart goat's cheese, with interleaving layers of a zesty salsa and a thickened apricot mousse.

Inwardly proud of his starter choice and its impeccable presentation, Stefano also subtly observed the reactions of the guests as they slowly relished the combined tier.

The second course, a small bowl of elderflower and lemon sorbet topped with a sprig of spearmint, was then placed before the guests to reawaken their taste buds in readiness for the main course.

Between courses, the diligent waiters returned to stand beside the head chef, silently anticipating the diners' needs.

Conversation was lively and humorous as the champagne flowed freely, topped up as soon as each glass was emptied.

Several times throughout the meal, he found it difficult to conceal his love for his wife and, at every opportune moment, he'd take hold of her hand and lean in to kiss her.

For the main course, the guests were served a perfectly-formed golden oblong of crispy pan-seared seabass, balanced on a square bed of saffron-infused sweet potato and topped with a spiced coconut and lime dressing.

Conversation ceased, except for the gustatory onomatopoeic murmurs of mmm's and ooh's, as every portion of food on each plate was devoured.

After the table was cleared and before the dessert was served, all the guests contributed to the customary delivery of speeches, each congratulating the newly-wed couple.

Stefano glanced in the direction of his head chef and the waiters promptly entered the room.

In the centre of each large round plate was a seamless sphere of white meringue, resting on a bed of dark chocolate shavings, accompanied by droplets of raspberry coulis.

As they cracked open the sphere with their spoons, a zesty filling of lemon and lime ice cream was exposed and more childish murmurs of delight echoed around the room.

Nick took charge of the music, whilst everyone danced energetically to hits of the 60's, 70's and 80's.

Once the guests had left, Alastair took her in his arms and whispered in her ear.

"Well, Mrs Brickman, would you like me to show you how much I love you?"

Giving him that knowing look, she beamed whilst thinking how Mrs Esme Brickman had a nice ring to it.

"I would."

twenty four

On the morning of 16th July, the residents of Chancel Quarter and twelve members of the family whose ancestors were buried in the chantry, all assembled for a service which was to be held by a local priest.

Having already received a visit from Stefano and Camellia, to explain how the ancient ruins had been renovated, he'd offered to conduct a small thanksgiving service in honour of Our Lady of Mount Carmel.

On arrival, he was pleasantly surprised with the efforts that had been made. The last time he'd viewed the crumbling remains, was when the family had duly informed him about the sale of the properties and surrounding land.

Candles were lit and placed within the chantry on each side of the makeshift altar covered in a white cloth. Also on the altar, from where the priest would deliver his service, was a statue of Our Lady and a vase of white roses.

Everyone listened intently, as they learnt about the history of how a community of monks lived on Mount Carmel and how, despite a succession of difficulties hindering the progress, the community had built a church and a monastery in 1263 which was dedicated to the Virgin Mary. They also discovered how the first feast day was celebrated in the latter part of the 14th century and the wearing of the brown scapular and how it shows a commitment to following Jesus and his will.

The priest duly informed them of a Carmelite prayer and hymn, *Flos Carmeli*, which meant Flower of Carmel. It had been written by Saint Simon Stock when he'd prayed to the Blessed Mother for help during difficult times.

Asking his audience to reflect on the meaning of the words, he opened his prayer book and read from it.

To close the service, Camellia's soprano voice echoed around the chantry as she sang 'Ave Maria' in Latin.

Unexpectedly, a gentle breeze wafted past them and Esme sensed a spiritual presence. Perhaps it was a sign of acknowledgement and gratitude for all of the restoration work which had been so lovingly undertaken.

Following a brief speech, she presented the lovingly-compiled photo album to the descendants of the White House. Before and after snapshots of the chantry renovation were included, as were images of everyone involved. It would serve as a keepsake to be passed down to generations.

twenty five

After hanging around outside for a few hours, he'd taken the opportunity to sneak in when a worker had left the outside door open.

Hiding underneath the deep stairwell, behind a storage cupboard in the reception area, he'd waited vigilantly and spied his chance. He grinned as he read the notice in bold lettering.

STRICTLY IMPORTANT

REMEMBER TO CHECK THAT THIS
DOOR IS SECURELY CLOSED
WHEN YOU LEAVE THE BUILDING

The external door slammed shut and the internal door flung open. The abrupt noise made everyone jump, including him.

"Yeah, I've got what we need. It's ok. I had one in the van."

Stealthily, the intruder edged his way towards the door. Peeking through the square glass panel, he glimpsed a small group of tradesmen gesturing animatedly whilst taking measurements. Trembling, he waited for the right moment.

Checking the deep pocket in his tatty overcoat, he nodded. It was still there.

Most of the group, except one man, dispersed into another room. Could it be that his luck was in this time? He'd tried before, but there'd been too many people around.

Spying his chance, he slowly opened the door, holding it tightly so it wouldn't slam. On tiptoes, he crept into the room, watching and waiting for the right moment. Fortunately, his tatty baseball boots, which usually squeaked, didn't announce his arrival.

The floor felt soft and bouncy and his steps were unsteady. The opportunity had finally arrived. It would definitely happen this time. Dead right, it would! There was no chance of him escaping.

He stopped and reached into his pocket again. Yes, it was still there.

Nearly losing his balance, his boots squeaked on the tiled floor.

Taken unawares, Alastair turned around, alarmed to see him there. The drawings fell onto the floor.

"Hey, you, dickhead. What yer lookin at? Yer think I'm a scruffy get, don't ya? Yer always did."

Alastair leant back against the kitchen units and folded his arms.

"Hello. How did you get in?"

"Through the fuckin door. How the fuck d'ya think I gorrin?"

The loud sounds of the workmen, drilling and banging in the next room, made it difficult to hear what he was saying.

"Never mind how I gorrin. I want youse to tell me why yer not gonna let me stay 'ere in this place."

Explaining why his application had been rejected, he could see that the man was high on drugs and tactfully attempted to diffuse the situation.

"I do understand you being angry, but we've

taken advice from the support workers and there are not many rooms available. Maybe it'll be your chance next time."

Alastair had spoken with the man on several occasions, when he'd been sheltering with Ali in the doorways. He'd previously begged for one of the rooms, but it wasn't feasible. Due to his complex and challenging behaviour issues, he was too high a risk.

He speculated on how he'd had managed to enter the secure building and, as the adrenaline pumped through his veins, he could hear the banging sound of his own rapid heartbeats.

Attempting to control the quaking which took over his body, he watched fearfully as the intruder fumbled in his pocket before edging towards him.

"Yer understand! Yer understand! Don't tell me ya fuckin understand. What the hell would you fuckin understand about living on the fuckin streets, eh? What would you know about fuckin drugs messing with yer 'ed? Fuckin Jack shit, that's what! Yer know fuckin nothin mate, with ya fancy clobber and ya fuckin flash car and yer fuckin posh voice."

The drilling continued and the man's resentful rantings quickened. His shoulders were moving up and down and his head was shifting from side to side, as he struggled to balance himself. His hand moved over his scraggly beard and Alastair noticed his lips tightening.

"I've been waitin to get ya for a long time." I've seen ya, talking to Ali. Givin him money and scran. Yer never gave me any, did ya? Ya didn't even know I was there, 'cept for when I was pesterin ya, when yer sed Ali had a place 'ere. I always sed I'd get yer."

Leaning forward, the man repeatedly pointed his finger. Alastair edged away from him, his heart now beating faster and his muscles tightening, as he tried to attract the workmen's attention.

"Let's talk this through, shall we?"

"Hey you, al arse. Where yer goin?"

Hesitant with his reply, his mouth went dry and under his breath he prayed. A buzzing in his ears made him feel dizzy and his vision was blurred. He felt numb.

"Please God, help me."

"I sed, where yer goin?"

"Nowhere."

"I've got youse now, avn't I? Here's me, I aven't gorra carrot and look at youse, Mr Rich Man, hoity toity privileged get."

Alastair was about to make a run for it when he saw the man pull a knife out of his pocket. He froze as his unstable attacker quickly approached him, ready to lunge at him. Raising both of his hands in petrified surrender, he thought his attacker might back away.

A workman appeared.

"Hey, what are doing with that knife, mate?"

Taken off his guard, he pointed the knife at the man and moved forward, his entire body vibrating with venomous energy.

"Come 'ed. I'm ready for ya. You'll gerrit too, if ya come near me."

Panicking, the scared workman retreated to seek help.

Everything seemed to be happening in slow motion. As Alastair's legs began to shake involuntarily, an intense rush of dread pumped furiously through his body as he stared into the dark and threatening eyes.

In a split second, he could see the man lunging at him, the knife aimed at his upper chest. As Alastair tried to dodge him, he tripped on a trailing cable which was attached to a power tool and his irate attacker pounced. The weapon missed his chest but pierced deep into his arm. Dropping to the floor, with the knife insitu, he banged his head as he fell.

Two workmen came bounding in and wrestled the frenzied attacker to the ground. They restrained him whilst someone rang for the police.

"Gerroff me, yer fuckin bastards. Fuckin leave me alone. Ya doin me 'ed in. Gerroff me."

Another workman immediately grabbed some kitchen roll and wrapped it around the knife, ensuring that it wasn't dislodged.

The room was spinning. Alastair thought he was going to pass out. Dazed and gasping for breath, he remained faintly aware that more help had arrived.

His attacker was still ranting and threatening everyone, as he struggled to get free.

"Nice one. Why d'ya call the bizzies, eh?"

Two policemen took charge of the situation and, lifting him from within the stronghold of the two tradesmen, they escorted him outside and into the police car.

Two paramedics were knelt at the side of Alastair, checking his pulse and asking him numerous questions.

"Come on. Let's get you out of here."

After carefully lying him down on a stretcher and placing a blanket over him, they put a drip into his arm. One paramedic pressed on the wound just below the knife, to stem the bleeding, whilst the other checked his temperature, his breathing and his pulse.

Every nerve in his body was shaking and his teeth were chattering uncontrollably, as he reflected on the unexplainable edgy feeling he'd experienced earlier in the day, when a nagging nausea had invaded his stomach.

twenty six

He was taken straight into the triage unit where a doctor and two nurses were waiting. A policeman was already waiting outside, ready to take a statement.

Again, everything was surreal for Alastair.

He wasn't aware that he'd been taken to the x-ray department for a scan, to determine the extent of the soft tissue injury.

"Mr Brickman. Can you hear me? We'll need to take you to theatre. It's a bad wound you have there."

Those were the last words he heard until he woke up in the recovery ward, feeling lightheaded and bewildered

As he lay there, the bright overhead lights hurt his eyes and he closed them. His outstretched arm felt heavy. Opening his eyes again, he saw that he was attached to several wires leading to a machine.

"You've been lucky, Mr Brickman. I've sutured the lacerations to your muscles and your skin."

He nodded drowsily.

"I've prescribed intravenous medication for the pain and some strong antibiotics. You've also had a tetanus injection. You're going to be ok."

His eyelids felt heavy.

"Your wife's waiting outside. Would you like to see her?"

He struggled to keep his eyes open and drifted off. He didn't even have the strength to speak.

When Esme had received the telephone call from one of the tradesmen, she had instantly felt nauseous. Although she appeared calm on the outside, she was trembling on the inside.

With panic overpowering her senses and her heart thrashing wildly inside her chest, she'd prayed fervently as she drove unconsciously competent, along the M62 motorway into the centre of Liverpool. Her feet were juddering on the pedals. The way she felt, she knew she shouldn't have been driving, but she had to get to him! She'd lost one husband and she didn't want to lose this one, too! The sat-nav had directed her to the hospital and, luckily, there was an empty parking space.

She'd been taken into a side room, where a nurse informed her about him going to theatre. After a lengthy wait, she was escorted to the recovery ward, where she'd sat for an hour holding his hand, waiting for him to wake up.

He opened his eyes and saw her.

"Hello darling. How are you?"

Sighing, she squeezed his hand and smiled.

"I'm ok. You?"

He smiled.

"Still a bit woozy. My mouth's so dry. Do you think it might be the anaesthetic? Could I have some water please?"

A nurse came over and moistened his lips with a piece of wet gauze, before checking his levels on the monitor.

"How are you feeling, Alastair?"

"As if I'm on another planet. I'm not in any pain though. Could I just have a drink? I'm thirsty."

"Not yet. We don't want you to be sick. We'll try you with some water when we take you up to the surgical ward."

An hour later, Esme followed the hospital trolley up to the ward where he would be staying. She wanted to ask him so many questions, but he was 'out of it'. The triage nurse had informed her of what had happened, but she wanted to hear his version.

It was 10.30pm when they arrived on the ward and after reassuring her that he was ok, the nurse had advised her not to stay too long.

Without words, she gently squeezed his hand as he drifted into sleep.

twenty seven

Alastair woke up with the words ringing in his ears, 'What would you fuckin know'? The comment had touched a nerve.

Agitated, he reflected on his choice of words when he'd calmly told his attacker that he understood. Obviously, dealing with his own stuff, his attacker saw the world with different eyes and would have felt patronised.

After eating a slice of toast, he sat in a high-back chair at the side of his bed and absent-mindedly flicked through a woman's magazine which someone had left on the bedside cabinet.

Glancing up, he saw a policeman enter the ward. Deducing the officer was coming to speak to him, he carried on reading.

"Hello, Mr Brickman. How are you feeling this morning? You were very lucky, weren't you?"

He nodded. That was the second time he'd been told that.

"Just want to get a statement from you. Then we have it on record for later for the court case."

Alastair relayed the details of the incident.

"What court case? I haven't said that I want to press charges, have I?"

"It's a serious offence, Mr Brickman. He'll be charged with possession of a dangerous weapon and grievous bodily harm. I can see you're still somewhat confused, so I'll give you a call in a few days and we can talk again."

"Ok. Thanks."

Not wanting to make conversation with the other patients, he drew the curtains around him and sat there, constantly self-interrogating and not making any real sense of what had happened to him.

Why hadn't he seen it coming? He'd heard the man chunnering when he was with Ali, but he hadn't taken much notice of what he'd been saying. Had he failed to recognise his threats? At the time, he just thought they were the ramblings of a drunken man.

His attacker was right though. What would he know? He'd been very fortunate to have never been in that situation. How could he understand?

He knew that he lived in a comfortable home, ate healthy and ample food, wore clean clothes and had a hefty bank balance and other assets.

He also had a respectable business and reliable friends. He was conscious that he didn't have to beg on the streets to find money to feed a habit. He recognised that he wasn't fully aware of how the homeless people actually felt. How could he know? He'd never experienced living on the streets.

His thoughts remained with him until Esme came to visit in the afternoon. She'd been texting him all morning, asking how he was. Even though he'd replied, his texts were short. His mind was elsewhere.

"You should really consider pressing charges, Alastair. He may do it to someone else."

"Es, I don't want to. I've thought about it all morning. I just want to give him a chance to turn his life around. I saw him once with a little girl. She was holding his hand and looking up at him. I somehow thought it could have been his daughter. I just kept thinking of how she'd feel about her dad if he was jailed. The man needs some help, to sort out his mental health."

He'd given her a glimpse of his feminine side when he'd spoken about the girl. Esme would have liked to have had a daughter of her own!

"Es. I've just remembered Ali saying the man's name was Ollie. "

Ali told him that his wife had cheated on him. He'd used alcohol and drugs to numb the pain and his addictions continued to spiral out of control.

From that perspective, he'd a good idea of how he'd be feeling. When Jen had cheated on him and left him, he'd also felt as though he was going crazy.

"Can I tell you something, Es? I had a vivid dream the other night. I was being stabbed in the heart by someone and I was bleeding to death. The man looked a little like me when I was younger. It was so strange. I could smell my mother's perfume and I could feel the touch of her hand on mine. She whispered in my ear, "Look after him, Alastair." I can usually control what happens in my dreams, but this time I was drifting towards my death, until I suddenly woke up, sweating profusely. How ironic is that?"

Observing the anguish on her husband's ashen face, she tightly gripped his trembling hand and focused on infusing her healing energy into him. A part of his predictive dream had unexpectedly come true!

twenty eight

Having remained in the hospital for two more days, Alastair was more than eager to leave.

Following the doctor's visit to check on his progress, he was discharged, with specific instructions to keep his dressing dry and to return a week later to the clinic.

On the journey home, he tried to divert the conversation towards his self-build clients. Anything to take his troubled mind off what had happened. He'd also offered silent prayers to God, thanking him for his life.

It was only as Esme's car came to a halt on the driveway, that he realised his own car was still parked on the office premises. He wouldn't be able to drive it for a while anyhow, so at least it would be safe in the gated premises.

Lifting the bin bag out of the boot, containing the clothes he was wearing when he was attacked, she took it inside and placed it in the utility room. So certain that he wouldn't want to wear it again, she'd dispose of the contents later.

Feeling weak, he sat on the sofa, so glad to be in his own home.

She prepared a light lunch and placed it before him.

After picking at the food on his plate, his mind returned to the attack.

"I couldn't taste that food then, Es. Can you turn that music off please? I can't seem to concentrate with it on. There's a ringing in my ears."

They sat for a while in silence. Then, out of the blue, he opened a conversation.

"What the majority of people don't realise is that homelessness could happen to anyone. One minute your life is ok and the next minute it's in turmoil.

I knew a businessman whose wife had left him because he was so hooked on gambling and seducing other women. He'd put his house up as collateral to feed his habit and when it became excessively out of control, the debtors foreclosed and took the house. He turned to the bottle for comfort and he'd lost everything, including his wife and his sons.

With nowhere to go, he started to drink, living in the alleyways. I saw him several times and he told me that living on the streets was all he was fit for. Later, he moved to a different city, because he so embarrassed that people would recognise him when he was in his drunken stupor. Most of his benefits went on alcohol.

He'd managed to get some therapy, but the demon returned and then he was on a swift downward spiral. The rehabilitation centre had done everything possible to help him, but he found it difficult to cope without alcohol. The last time I saw him, he told me he'd had a premonition that he'd die on the streets. He did. It was another life lost."

"How sad. How did you get to know him?"

He bowed his head and sighed.

"That man was my dad. We didn't even know that he had died. He must have felt as if no one cared about him. It was only when someone read about him and saw his photo in the paper, that we found out. We couldn't afford a decent funeral for him. He had a pauper's funeral and we put a wooden cross where we'd buried his ashes. His death haunted me for years. It still does, to a certain degree. I felt I could have done more to help him, but I was still at college and, because we'd nowhere else to go, having lost our home, we lodged with my grandma. We'd gone from living a most luxurious lifestyle to my mum sleeping on the sofa, whilst myself and my brother slept in the second bedroom."

Moving closer, she placed her arm around his shoulder and carefully pulled him closer.

"Before my dad's misfortune, I hadn't really given much thought to homelessness. It was just there, on nearly every street corner in the town centres and cities. After he'd died it really got to me. Obviously, not enough though, because I just got on with my life and tried to block it out; pretending it wasn't there. It was only when I met Ali, that it hit me again."

Alastair hadn't intended to cause Esme any discomfort, by spontaneously disclosing fragments of his earlier life.

"Sorry, Es for going on like that. I don't know where all that came from. Could you pass me a tissue, please?"

"It's ok."

By encouraging him to talk about his dad, she'd learnt so much more about his consciously forgotten experiences and feelings, understanding a little more about why he didn't want to press charges. His caring side was coming to the forefront, especially when he'd spoken about Ollie's little girl. It was as if the little girl had taken on a parental role and Alastair's attacker was the child.

"I remember how my dad was always working away. Sometimes for a year at a time. He'd ring to see how we were. I missed him. When he was at home, I'd hear him speaking to other women on the phone, all lovey-dovey! I'd never once heard or saw him being affectionate with my mum. I don't know how she put up with him for so long."

"Maybe she loved him, in her own way."

Alastair didn't think so. He'd never seen any love shown between them.

"You don't mind me talking, do you?"

"No. Carry on. I'm interested in what you have to say."

He rubbed his ears several times. The buzzing noise was irritating him.

"When I think about it, there were similarities in my own marriage. I don't mean the women. I mean the way in which I put my work first. Is work more important than family? Is money more important than family?"

Whilst he waited for her answer, she raised her eyebrows and shrugged.

"When I think about it, Jen must have been as lonely as my mum had been! No wonder she looked for company elsewhere."

She speculated if his marriage had been strong enough and whether he'd been content with working away from home for lengthy periods. Remembering how she was desperate for Leo to come back from his occasional working trips abroad, she also recalled their enthusiastic lovemaking on his return and his endless devoted attention towards her.

"My dad's experience left a permanent scar on me. I vowed I'd never end up that way. I remember him saying to me that he'd let us down and that he was sorry. He had no hope, Es. He must have felt he'd nothing to live for."

Seeing that he was tiring and sensing his wistfulness, she handed him a glass of water.

"So, when Jen left me, I could have easily ended up like him, losing my business and my self-esteem. I couldn't have done it. My mum had worked day and night to put me through university. She died soon after I'd graduated. I didn't get the opportunity to help her, like she'd helped me."

She handed him the box of tissues and waited.

Clearing his throat, he continued.

"I couldn't have taken the same path as him. When I think about it, Es, my father's downfall had been an incentive for me to succeed. It was also what got me through the dark days when Jen left. I wasn't going to allow history to repeat itself."

She could see he'd been dealing with his own darkness for far too long. The way he'd opened up had been healing for him. He'd bottled it up for all those years. It had emerged again when Jen had left, but he'd dealt with it in a way which he thought was best. Again, she understood a little more about his reasons for not pressing charges. In an odd way, because of the stabbing, his attacker had caused him to introspect on his past. However, it didn't allay her fears. The vicious attack on her husband was tantamount to attempted murder; even if the man was high on drugs and alcohol.

"I still feel guilty about my dad's death. I often wonder if I could have done more to help him. I did try to talk to him, but he pushed me away. His life was in the bottle."

Aware that by trying to fix things for him, she could possibly make it worse, she offered her advice anyhow.

"Try not to feel that way. You were not responsible for the actions of your father. Helping some is better than helping no one. You've already made a difference, supporting Ali and facilitating with the setting up of Habitaire. Don't beat yourself up about it. You can't bring the past back."

He began to visibly shake and she held onto him tightly. The shock of the attack had left him as weak as a kitten.

"I know I'm on antibiotics, but do you think I could have a small brandy?"

"Of course, I'll put some lemonade in it. You should be ok."

His mind returned to the attack. His life could have ended in a split second. By exploring the inner depths of his subconscious, he deduced that someone must have been looking after him. Could it have been his mum, or even his dad?

twenty nine

She'd monitored her husband closely, watching for any mood swings. His once-confident persona had swiftly changed and he was now a vulnerable man who was experiencing sporadic breathing difficulties, needing constant reassurance.

His subdued silence was only to be expected. The incident had not only exhausted his body; it had also exhausted his mind. He was too weary to talk or even think!

Two days after leaving the hospital, the police had phoned him. Again, he reiterated that he was not going to press charges, because he knew that he'd tripped over a cable as his attacker was approaching him and, anyway, he couldn't be sure that the man would have actually attacked him.

They couldn't understand his reason and asked if there were any underlying or conflicting issues which they should know about. He'd informed them that his attacker obviously had mental health issues and had been high on drugs and alcohol when it happened and wasn't fully in control of what he was doing. He'd also told them that he'd refused the man a place in the homeless centre, due to him not being ready to live independently and responsibly.

Alastair had his own reasons for not wanting to press charges and was satisfied with his decision. Others didn't need to understand his reasons. It wasn't their journey. He didn't want his attacker to go to prison. He only wanted to give him a chance. He'd witnessed the demise of people's mental health many times throughout his career, including his own.

Esme had stayed at home with him for several days, only leaving the house to collect food and to attend a couple of pre-arranged meetings, which she was unable to cancel.

One afternoon, after returning from shopping, she found him fully clothed, asleep on the bed. His legs were drawn up to his chest in a foetal-like position and he was hugging his pillow tightly.

Leaving him to rest, she started work on some designs in her study area.

She heard him disturb and walked into the bedroom. He was sat on the edge of the bed with his head in his hands.

"Alastair. What's the matter?"

"I feel so dizzy. The room is spinning and when I tried to stand up, I lost my balance. My legs feel weak."

"Just lie down again and rest."

"I can't. I feel as if I want to be sick."

She handed him a glass of water and as he took the glass, it slipped out of his hand and fell on the floor. Luckily, it didn't smash.

"Sorry, Es. I don't seem to have any strength in my arms or my hands. Everything seems blurred."

His speech was garbled and he looked dazed.

"Lie down, Alastair."

She lifted his feet and lay his limp body on the bed. Grabbing her phone, she dialled the emergency number.

"I think he's had a stroke. I don't know what to do. Can you send someone quickly?"

Within ten minutes, the buzzer sounded and

she pressed the button to open the gates, which would allow the ambulance to enter.

Two paramedics rushed up the stairs, asking several questions as they went.

They could see the dressing on his arm and as they set about examining him, Esme quickly relayed what had happened.

"What's this bruise on his head?"

"When he was attacked, he fell and banged his head."

He was aware that other people were there and was confused as to why someone other than Esme was talking to him.

"Can you hear me, Alastair?"

"Yes, I can. Who are you? What are you doing here?"

"I'm a paramedic. I'm just checking you over. You haven't been well, have you?"

He shook his head and then held the palm of his hand on the top of his head.

"What's happening? My head's throbbing."

She stood back and anxiously watched as the paramedics were undertaking several tests on her husband.

"From examining him, we can see he hasn't had a stroke. His symptoms are a combination of his attack and bang to the head. It's what we call Post-Concussion Syndrome. It doesn't necessarily reveal itself straight away after an injury. It can take a bit longer."

Exhausted, both physically and emotionally, she exhaled a long, drawn-out sigh and struggled to hold back her tears.

"I'm so glad to hear that. I didn't know what to

think or do. I was so scared."

"It was wise of you to ring, but I can reassure you that he hasn't had a stroke. It's usually only a temporary thing, but if his symptoms get worse, don't hesitate to ring us immediately."

"Thank you very for coming out so quickly. Can he take any medication for his headache? He's on antibiotics."

"Yes. He can take Paracetamol. Do you have any? It shouldn't cause any problems. Just keep an eye on him."

"Yes."

As she showed the paramedics out, their eyes were on stalks as they scanned the space.

"Nice gaff, you have here, love."

She smiled.

As the ambulance neared the gates, she pressed the remote and returned upstairs.

Frustrated and frightened for her husband's health, she lay motionless beside him as he slept and allowed her fears to flow down her cheeks.

thirty

His internal conflict had manifested itself in numerous ways.

In his sleeping dreams, he could see images of his mother, father, brother and aunt smiling at him. He could see himself angrily shouting at them for dying before he'd had the chance to say goodbye. Visions of him organising their funerals and walking behind the coffins, disturbed him. His father was a permanent feature in every emotionally-charged recall.

In following his own path, his father's addictive work ethic, his inclination to chase fame and money and his insatiable hunger to succeed at any cost, had led to the downfall of his marital relationship and his parental relationship with his children.

Alastair recollected how his father had told him endless stories about his grandfather and great-grandfather who were both architects and how they too possessed the same traits.

On other occasions, like someone who'd been suddenly woken from a heavy sleep, he'd rub his eyes and blink several times and contemplate heavily on his intentionally-suppressed memories.

Unknowingly, his subconscious mind had been analysing and connecting the accumulated behaviours of his ancestral past, with his own obviously repetitive and shared inherited traits of also being determined to achieve at whatever cost.

During reflective moments, he'd close his eyes and he'd endure chaotic visions of being confronted by his attacker's contorted face and a knife piercing into him. Even after he opened his eyes, he couldn't escape the lingering foetid odour of a possible premature death.

He had visions of his ex-wife having sex with her lover and they were both laughing at him. At that time, when he'd woken, he felt embarrassed when Esme had said he'd been shouting and swearing.

Embedded also in his psyche, was his father's lack of interest in doing things with him. The words he'd said and hadn't said, had lain heavy within in his heart. Although he'd never challenged him when he was alive, Alastair now wished he had done.

On occasions, he'd go for walks with Esme, but mostly he walked alone through the open land at the back of the house, always ending up in the chantry. He'd sit on one of the benches, pondering on recent events and his future. He didn't want her to see the state he was in.

She'd encouraged him to keep a journal so he could write down his innermost thoughts and desires. Journalling had become a daily habit, as well as sketching and reading. Some of the fiction books he'd previously acquired, but hadn't read, had also transported him to other places, suitably distracting him from his perturbation.

It was nearing the end of the first week of his release from hospital that she'd heard him raise his voice.

Once more, he'd been connecting with the incident, desperately trying to analyse why it had happened.

During a casual conversation, she'd unwisely queried his irrational reasoning and his decision not to generate charges against his attacker. He hadn't anticipated her uninvited question. Neither had she anticipated his impulsive outburst!

Following their heated words, she'd cautiously decided a more subtle approach was required. Mindful of his inner and external pain, she'd remained silent, remembering that it wasn't her purpose to 'fix him'.

Although weary from the events of the last few days, she'd tried to remain sensitive to his fragile situation; discerning that she'd have to trust that he'd manifest his own help and that he'd find his own answers.

At that moment, she'd speculated on whether his recent traumatic experience, combined with his personal and collective consciousness, would inspire him to clear past negative episodes.

As she pondered on the old adage, 'Love Thy Enemies' and how we somehow attract them, she hoped that they'd both be able to extend some love to the man who had carried out the attack!

thirty one

Earlier in the day, he'd attended the hospital for the third time since the attack occurred.

Later, after they'd eaten dinner, they sat on the sofa listening to Bach. She'd constantly played the composer's music when she'd been studying and had found his work to have a calming and soothing effect on her. Appreciating how the concertos had a spiritual tone to them, she hoped they'd have the same effect on Alastair.

"I know I keep going on about it, Es, but I'm repeatedly reliving the attack in my mind. It terrified me, you know. I keep breaking out in a cold sweat and then I start shaking."

In his mind's eye, he could see himself falling forward onto the knife and he speculated again on whether his attacker would have stabbed him; or was he just trying to frighten him. He was unsure.

She placed her hand on his thigh, reassuringly.

"Why do you think I keep going back to the precise moment? It just comes over me. Memories of when I was at university, when someone jumped me from behind, also keep flooding back. He'd split my head open with just one punch and there was loads of blood everywhere. I didn't know the guy. He legged it and my friends took me to the hospital."

A sudden stab in her chest took her breath away. She didn't like seeing him suffer.

"Alastair, the attack has left you traumatised. Your mind is trying to process it."

"Sorry if I keep going on about it. I just need to talk. I'm sorry for being irritable and distant."

She placed her finger on his lips. Nothing more needed to be said. Then placing her hand on his cheek, she left it there for a few moments. His distant gaze penetrated her anxious heart and her inner emotional awareness again experienced his own psychological suffering.

Her mind went back to the times when her mother used to tell her to count to ten, before saying anything which she thought might not be deemed necessary. She offered her advice anyhow.

"You don't have to say sorry. There's strength in being honest about how you're feeling. Showing your vulnerability is not a sign of weakness. It's so important that you talk about it."

The words 'vulnerability' and 'weakness' were not part of his vocabulary. It wasn't what he was about!

Again, he apologised.

"Sorry, Es. It's been all about me, hasn't it? It's just that I've been in another dimension for the past week. I haven't even thought to ask how you are feeling."

Looking away from his gaze, she lied. Since his outburst, she'd cared for him with compassion and gentle words but, in all honesty, she was physically and mentally sapped.

"I'm good, thanks. We just need to get you well again."

The attack had affected her too, but she needed to remain strong for him. Trying to detach herself was difficult and she had to concede that his attack had also been a serious shock to her system.

Her depleted energy was overwhelming at times, but she knew that if she didn't remain in control of her emotions, they'd suffocate her. He didn't need to see her blubbering whilst he was trying to deal with his own issues. Determined to aid his recovery, she wouldn't allow her distress to become a burden for him.

Whilst she'd been attempting to subtly and sensitively rebuild his confidence, she was also fully aware that she'd been neglecting herself, functioning on automatic pilot.

During meditative moments, she'd been asking her spirit guide to direct her through the trauma. His answer had been, "Push ahead. All is as it should be. You'll see."

That's what she was doing, pushing through the tough stuff. Alastair, more so than her, would have to go through it to come out at the other side! Her job was to support him, guide him and love him. She was a past master at that. She'd drawn on every ounce of strength when she'd administered similar care to Leo. Towards the end of his life, her first husband's demise had been heartbreaking to witness and dreadfully difficult for her to endure, even though her copious capacity to deal with the situation had been admired by her family and friends.

Leo had always said that his life, without her in it, would be so empty and uninspiring. Her immense strength had been gained through her own suffering and heartache.

Thankful that Alastair's physical symptoms seemed to be easing somewhat, if not his emotional torment for now, she didn't want to think of what her life would be like now, if he wasn't in it!

thirty two

After returning from an early morning meeting with a client, she'd been sitting at the kitchen island updating records. Discreetly, she'd observed him shredding endless reams of unwanted paperwork and sorting through a pile of old photographs, which he'd laid in even in piles over the floor.

A strong maternal feeling came over her and she wondered what it would have been like if they had met earlier. Would they have had children? Who would the baby have looked like? Would it have had his features? Would it be a boy or a girl? She wanted to wrap her husband in a shawl and nurse away his fears.

Stepping down from the stool, she sat beside him and kissed him. His usual clean-shaven face was now darkened with stubble and it gave him a rugged look which she quite liked. The bruise was still visible on his temple. Her soft fingertips touched the black and blue patch as she patted some arnica gel on it to help with the bruising.

"How was your morning?"

"It was ok, thanks. My colleague rang again to see how I was feeling. He's still going on about me pressing charges."

"That was nice of him. He is only concerned for you."

He picked up a tin box and proceeded to flick through some old black and white photographs of his family.

"This one is when we all went on holiday to America. We travelled to Pennsylvania and went to look at a magnificent house called Fallingwater. It had two overhanging balconies and a waterfall beneath it. See, here I am with my brother, Angus. My parents kept a close eye on us. They thought we might fall over the edge."

She took hold of the faded photograph and examined it closely. His brother had similar features to him. In fact, they could have been twins. There was only eighteen months between them; Angus being the elder. Alastair's features hadn't changed that much. In fact, he'd become even more even more attractive with age.

"I've seen photos of this building before in design journals. It's spectacular. What's it like inside?"

"It's breathtaking, Es. The house gives you the impression that it's not built on any solid ground. Wherever you were in the house, you could always hear trickling water. I was so impressed with it, that I researched the architect who'd designed it. Frank Lloyd Wright was one of the reasons I became an architect. It's now a UNESCO world heritage site."

"I'd like to see it."

"You'd love it. I chose Wright as a subject for a dissertation. I can remember quoting how he was the greatest architect of the 20th century and that his buildings were far beyond the architecture of his time. I truly believe that he was!"

Enjoing listening to him talking about his interests, she clung onto his every word.

"I drew inspiration from all of his work. I was also influenced by Japanese architecture and its geometric designs."

"I can see that from the many commissions that you've already shown me."

"Wright also believed that every man, woman and child had the human right to live in beautiful circumstances and I always remember his influential words when I design houses."

> *"The mission of an architect is to help people understand how to make life more beautiful, the world a better one for living in and to give reason, rhyme and meaning to life."*

Alastair floated off into a pensive state.

Respecting his sudden need for silence, she sat and waited a while before Interrupting his quietude.

"Penny for your thoughts?"

"I miss Angus. He died a three years ago. He was a bit of a loner and never married. I just wish we'd spent more time together."

"Sometimes life gets in the way. Time passes so quickly. Our intentions fall by the wayside."

Agreeing with her sentiments, he nodded.

Only that morning, he thought of how much easier it would have been to stay in bed or lie on the sofa, with only his fears and insomnia for company. Instead, he'd persevered with his daily routine. Doing so, seemed to bring some welcome comfort to his befuddled mind.

"Another thing happened. Whilst I was at the chantry this morning, I felt as if someone or something was around me. I can't explain it, really."

"If you felt it, perhaps there was."

"I'd ventured out for my usual meander, just connecting with nature and pulling up the sprouting weeds from around the gravestones. I sat down for a few minutes on one of the benches, just watching the sun filter its way through the trees. It was casting shadows through the stained-glass window and I was totally mesmorised by it. It was ever so serene. The remnants of the early morning dew were glistening on the field. The air had been still and then I felt a gentle breeze. A dove flew over my head. Where did that come from? I couldn't believe it. I must admit, I started praying, like I did when I was a little boy with my hands joined."

He thought of how, whilst sitting amongst the ghosts in the chantry, he'd channeled the ghosts of his own life and that of his family. He often wondered why he hadn't detected his parent's discontentment. Why he hadn't even noticed his brother's propensity for secrecy regarding his emerging homosexuality. The accumulated pain of his father's behaviour and the tragic way his life had ended, still haunted him in a suffocating way. It also made him question whether he could have been much more supportive towards them.

He recalled many cherished memories of his mother's unceasing love and how she always said how she idolised 'her boys'. He missed her. Sorely!

Listening attentively, she was familiar with the language of signs and synchronicity. She knew it was a communication for him; an awakening.

"I was well aware that I was asking for reasons, answers and meanings, when maybe I just needed to figure them out for myself."

Intrigued, she nodded.

"I could hear a man's voice talking to me, Es.

When I looked around there was no one there and yet the presence was palpable. It was as if someone was sat on the bench at the side of me."

Alastair took a few deep breaths and his hand reached for hers.

"I questioned why it was with me. It said that I couldn't change all the things that had happened to me. I needed to deal with it and move on."

He knew then, that his attack was beyond his control and he had to accept it.

Absorbed, she waited for more details.

"He also said, 'Listen to your soul. Don't allow yourself to become a victim. You should love your enemy because it is they that need it the most. Think about it. You're fortunate to be alive. The same thing happened to me, but I didn't survive'."

"So, you were having a private conversation with a spirit, then?"

"I suppose I was. I really wanted to ask it more questions, but the voice faded away. In my peripheral vision, I saw a shadowy outline walk away towards the gravestones and into a nothingness. After it had left, it was so bizarre. It was if I was trying to make peace with myself."

His experience didn't disturb her. Leo's spirit had been a constant in her life.

"My faith in God has returned. I suppose it has never really left me. I think it's been lying dormant, ever since things happened in my life and my prayers went unanswered, for whatever reasons. As the spirit said, what happened, happened. I've got to accept it!"

Unknowingly, his attacker had forced him to confront his hidden insecurities and demons. His recent otherworldly encounter had also had a most profound effect on him. He'd contemplated the meaning of 'oneness' and how we all have a part to play in others' lives and be of service to each other.

"I just sat there in a surreal space, holding the palm crystal you gave me and unravelling my own theory about the correlation between me, my father, Ali and my attacker."

Knowing the protective power of crystals, she'd given him a flat piece of black tourmaline to deflect the negativity he was experiencing. He carried it around with him, trusting that it would ease his overwhelming anxiety. She'd also placed a smooth piece of amethyst under his pillow to alleviate the recurring headaches he'd been experiencing.

He continued with his explanation of how he thought they all had unresolved issues.

"The common denominators, as I see it, are lack of love, poverty, homelessness and alcoholism. My dad hardly ever gave me any attention or showed me any love. I do remember him playing football with me once or twice, or giving me money to buy some clothes, but it wasn't the same as doing things with me and my brother. He was equally as neglectful with my mother. We did everything we could to please him, but nothing seemed to work. I'm sorry for repeating myself, Es."

He stopped for a moment, deliberating on that gloom-ridden period in his life. He contemplated on how his brother and his mother had perceived the situation. They hadn't talked about it much. They'd all just got on with it! They didn't have a choice!

"Ali also lacked love and attention you know, Es. He was destitute and homeless. Ollie's life was loveless. He too was an alcoholic, drug dependent, destitute and homeless. I do know that each person's suffering isn't the same, but ..."

She could see where he was coming from, as he poured his heart out.

"It seems so ironic that my dad used to ridicule the poor and the homeless and he ended up in the same position as them."

Somehow, she sensed that both his spiritual and emotional scars would take a little longer to heal, than the wound on his arm. His soul and his body had faced fresh challenges and he needed time to process things.

He picked up a photograph and handed it to her.

"Earlier, my mind went back to when I went on a walking holiday with my mates in the Lake District. That's why I was looking for the photo. There were five on us and we hired a cottage. We were in our twenties then and we all took turns cooking the evening meal."

"Bet that was fun."

He nodded.

"It wasn't a boozy holiday. We were all fitness fanatics and loved hiking. We had some fascinating discussions during and after our meals. They used to joke with me and call me Socrates, because I'd always argue my point on things and then ask them endless questions as to why they thought the way they did."

"Mmm! That *is* interesting. Socrates' motto was 'Know Thyself'. He believed that we needed to think for ourselves and that our true self is our soul, not our material wealth or our reputation. He wanted to achieve practical results for the well-being of society and he was always seeking to become a better person, by respecting all humans and by treating them with compassion."

"How are we supposed to know if our true self is our soul, though?"

She wondered where the conversation would lead to.

"We are our soul, Alastair. Socrates believed the soul is eternal and, when we die, it's not the end of existence. It's just that our soul separates from our body."

He didn't respond and she deduced that he was processing what she'd said.

"He further believed that through asking questions, the mind will find the absolute truth and that integrity was everything. Always questioning and avidly arguing his viewpoint, he was hungry for knowledge. He wasn't interested in other people's assumptions."

Silence ensued, as he tried to find another photo of himself and his mates climbing the hills.

"I'm sure it was in here. I'll find it."

She chuckled.

"Oh! Alastair. It's no wonder they called you Socrates. You always like to ask lots of questions."

He laughed with her and winked.

"Do I?"

"You know you do!"

When she'd told him about achieving practical results for the greater wellbeing of society, the words resonated with him. He surmised that his experience earlier was another step on his spiritual journey to self-actualisation.

Unable to find the photograph he wanted, he placed all of them back into the box.

"I'm going to try and get my life back on track.

The last few weeks have been difficult for me. I've been trying to clear my head from the damaging stuff."

He bent his head forward and scratched it with both hands.

"Are you managing it?"

"I'm getting there, I think. I keep encouraging myself to face my fears and accept what may be ahead for me. I've made a 'to do' list."

"Good."

Not wanting to probe further, she kissed him on his forehead and set about preparing the evening meal. She'd called in at the local fishmongers and an artisan bakery on the way home.

Busying herself, she slightly raised her head and watched him as he stood up and stared into the garden. The black shadows under his eyes and his recently stooped posture revealed much of what he'd been through.

She plated the sea bass with creamed fennel and some spicy carrots and called him over to the table. Opening a bottle of non-alcoholic Prosecco, she tipped the glasses as she poured the sparkling clear liquid into them.

"This looks nice, Es."

She hoped he'd eat all the food on his plate, this time.

"Yes. I thought we'd have a change. I know you like sea bass."

"Thanks, darling."

Over dinner, he spoke about his intentions. She was pleased to see an empty plate when he'd finished speaking. Hopefully, he was 'turning a corner'.

She raised her glass and toasted him.

"To you, Alastair and your visions."

Chinking her glass, he replied.

"To us. To us."

After eating a dessert of lemon tart with a quenelle of coconut ice cream, they sat closely on the sofa, listening to some of Bocelli's music. He revealed more of his determination not to let the unpredictable incident occupy his mind.

"This afternoon I asked myself what I should do now. I made the decision to retire. I'm going to sell my practice. The other guys in the office have spoken to me about it. They're repeatedly asking me how long I'd continue working. It suddenly dawned on me that there are more interesting things that I want to do with you."

Later that night as they lay in bed, she held him closer, infusing her energy into him, whilst he rested his head on her bare breasts.

"How do you feel about us both retiring, Es?"

"I think it's a great idea. Let's do it."

"What happened to me, has made me realise that there are only so many tomorrows and that life is such a precious gift."

The communication which he'd received had been instrumental to him making changes. The seeds of change had been sowed. His intention to retire was a part of his healing process.

He lifted his head up and kissed her.

"Can I show you something, Es?

She grinned.

"Can you?"

"I've missed you."

During the previous few weeks, he'd had no interest in making love. Rediscovering each other's erogenous zones, they breathlessly engaged in an energetic, passionate exchange of healing.

Totally satiated, they lay in each other's arms, just looking at each other. Densely concentrating, she stared into his eyes and, as he held her gaze, she could see the goodness in him. Even before the attack, despite his personal experiences, her husband had grasped the extent of people's suffering.

"What were you doing then, Es? I had a strange feeling."

"Just looking into your soul."

She discerned that life had given him his latest challenge to further his spiritual growth. He had responded by not pressing charges. It was his own journey. His choice. Others didn't need to understand his reason.

"Are you hungry? Those bedroom aerobics have given me an appetite. My headache's gone too."

"A little."

She wasn't that hungry, but she was pleased that he was and that his quirky sense of humour had returned. The heaviness that he'd been carrying with him appeared to have lifted.

Rotating his arm and his shoulder, he winced.

"Are you in pain?"

"A little. I'm going to begin exercising again. It'll make me feel better. The physio said I could start doing some slow, gentle stretching exercises."

"Well, I think that you've already raised your serotonin levels with the amount of exercise you've just had."

"I'll have to build my muscles up, if I'm going to be doing more of what I've just been doing."

Giggling, she playfully responded.

"You'd better do just that, then!"

"Thanks for giving me the space to work things out. This morning, I looked at what I'd lost in my life. Then I looked at what I have now. I have you and I'm so very grateful for that!"

Once more, she thought of how the attack had, unknowingly released something inside Alastair, which had been buried for years.

"Can I tell you something else?"

"Please do."

"Earlier, when I was walking through the fields, in my mind's eye, I could see me and you walking near the water's edge on a beach. I also keep dreaming about keys and locks. What do you think that's all about?"

Shrugging her shoulders, she smiled at him knowingly.

Their honeymoon was imminent. She also had her own visions for their future. The keys were also pertinent, in that they symbolised the handing over of the keys to his business and his house.

However, more importantly, the keys were a sign that he'd been courageous in unlocking the box, which had been holding all his dark memories; thereby setting them free.

thirty three

Sitting in the chantry, he surrendered himself to the silence and solitude. Even though the area was filled with the subtle sounds of nature, it was sublimely still and the air was fresh. He could hear his heart beating and a calming sensation engulfed him, as he gathered his thoughts and patiently waited for guidance.

Procrastination decided to pay him a visit again. Fortunately, it had only visited him on a few occasions throughout his life; the last time being when Jen had left him and the divorce had been finalised. In the aftermath of his recent adversity, the nagging whispering in his ear had, only last week, offered him some welcome comfort from his heavy workload. It was offering even more advice now.

"Wouldn't it be better if you had a few more weeks off, Alastair? Your clients won't mind. They'll understand. It's too soon to go back. You can stay here in this peaceful place, where no one will bother you. It's better for you."

Anticipation butted in.

"Don't listen. How much longer are you going to sit around and revisit past events? Those people are depending on you to complete their plans. Solitude can be healing, but interdependence is healing, too. You thrive on being with your clients and helping them. Think about it."

The two contradictory voices quietened.

Lifting his hand, he flicked it several times, as if shooing the voices away.

"I think both of you should go. I'll do what's right for me."

Following her lengthy stroll through the fields, Esme joined her husband on the bench.

"Who are you talking to, Alastair?

Startled by her appearance, he shook his head.

"Sorry, Es. I didn't hear you then. I've been talking to myself a lot lately."

Slightly nodding, she smiled.

"I know you have, darling. I've heard you."

"I'm still trying to get my head around things. I know I've said I want to retire, but it's a big step, isn't it?"

Wanting approval, he waited for her answer.

"I can't make that decision for you."

There'd been several times when she'd been tempted to offer advice, but she'd held her tongue.

His mind returned to the attack.

"Once the knife penetrated me, the fear of dying was so prominent in my mind. These last few weeks have made me re-evaluate my life. I know that impermanence is part of our existence and, from now on, I'm going to appreciate every single day. Hey, I don't know why I'm even thinking of changing my mind. I'm going to be the architect of my own life and construct my own future."

His assertive quip amused her, reminding her of how he was before the incident.

"I can't just sit here. I need to get back to my work. My clients are relying on me."

Common sense had prevailed. He'd listened to his intuition and was ready to return to work.

thirty four

Things were going swimmingly, apart from a telephone call from the police informing him that the Crown Prosecution were pressing ahead with the charges of assault against Oliver Anderson. Unquestionably, nothing could alter the fact that he'd committed a serious crime.

Alastair had briefly thought of how the name had sounded familiar.

It wasn't what Alastair wanted and, whilst he respected the law, it was obvious that the man had mental health issues and had been under the influence of drugs and alcohol.

Their retirement plans were well underway. All property contracts had been signed, exchanged and completed. Following negotiations with his employees, a decision was reached whereby three of them had bought the practice from him; on the proviso that they could continue using his name.

During a farewell meal at an Italian restaurant on the Royal Albert Dock in Liverpool, he was acknowledged by his staff for the many ways in which he'd delivered his own distinctive signature into architectural design. In doing so, he was mindful that he had provoked several cynical reactions from certain architects who preferred the more traditional style of structural construction. 'Each to his own' was his dictum.

Although contemporary was his preference, he'd also designed several traditional structures, in keeping with the Georgian and Victorian residences which graced the towns and cities throughout England.

When he was at university, he'd completed a thesis on the highly-acclaimed architect, Christopher Wren. Knowledge gained from that study had enabled him to fully understand the history of Georgian style and the rules for composition and design.

His sure confidence and proven success in this specific field, had resulted in him gaining awards from prestigious architectural institutes.

One award was for the design of a bespoke Georgian construction for an affluential client. That specific institute had been impressed with his balanced proportions and symmetry. His use of oversized hand-made bricks and locally-sourced stone, together with his geometric floor plans, uncluttered facades and elegant kerb-appeal had clearly demonstrated his expertise.

No. He was far from being a 'one-trick pony'!

His associates and staff also appreciated how he'd developed them, by encouraging each of them to stray from the expected, when expressing their own designs.

On Alastair's return to work, he'd learnt that Ali had waited every day in the same doorway hoping to see him.

Without hesitation, he'd immediately taken Ali to buy a mobile phone and arranged to pay his monthly bill, so he could keep in touch with him.

A week later, with some help from Alastairs contacts, Ali was temporarily living in a one-bedroom flat in a men's refuge until the accommodation at Habitaire was completed and then he'd move there. Alastair had opened a bank account for him, with the added promise of a monthly allowance being deposited in it, until he secured a job and was earning.

On one occasion, when Ali had rang him, he'd learnt that Ollie was now taking Methadone, he was attending all of his rehabilitation classes and was making good progress.

When thoughts of Ollie entered his head, he considered whether all humans possessed at least one form of addiction. He discerned that one of his fixations was exercise. Another had definitely been his unending devotion to his work!

thirty five

It had been nearly two months since the attack had occurred and Alastair had been in touch with his barrister friend, to explore the distinct possibility of not pressing charges, as opposed to what the police had stated.

Reliving the incident almost daily, he knew he couldn't possibly live with his conscience if he didn't do something about it.

Following a series of lengthy rationalisations and reiterations with the barrister, relating to the intense moments before he'd tripped over a trailing cable on the floor when the incident happened, he knew that he only had a vague recollection of what had happened.

He'd relayed how Ollie Anderson was in safe custody within a local rehabilitation hospital ward for assessment and detox therapy. He'd also informed him that Ollie, having no recollection of the incident, had found it hard to believe that he could have done such a thing. He hadn't been aware of his violent behaviour whilst under the power influence and had agreed to re-attend a Twelve Steps Recovery Programme. He'd attended on a previous occasion and, when it had proved too difficult for him, he'd sorely lapsed. This time he was determined to go through with it.

From a professional perspective, the case for prosecution had been fully discussed and, from the information which had been presented, his friend was sure there was a loophole to be found.

Following an extensive information-gathering exercise which included Alastair's police statement, a detailed report from the rehabilitation managers and numerous conversations with relevant contacts, he'd been pleased to receive a telephone call, informing him that a hearing would be imminent.

thirty six

On the day of the hearing, the court had learnt that it was Ollie's first offence and, after considering the complex set of circumstances, which detailed his dysfunctional background, they concluded that his early abandonment and ensuing adoption, his troubled teenage years and his failed marriage, had been contributory to his existing mental health and addictions. He was a damaged man!

Clouded by the insufficient evidence and the combination of uncertainty surrounding the incident, a decision was made that Alastair's attacker would fare better in rehabilitative environment. That would be a severe punishment in itself. Prison isn't designed to advance the recovery of those individuals who are substance dependent. Ollie would remain within a supportive environment, whist attending structured victim/offender mediation sessions, until the time came when it was deemed appropriate for him to live independently.

The lady judge had been professional yet understanding of the circumstances. Her husband had endured alcohol and drug addiction, so she was fully aware, first-hand, of the traumas involved and how society deemed this form of addiction as being a disease. In this case, and indeed her husband's situation, it was a destructive response to their past adversities and suffering.

His persistence had paid off. He'd only ever wanted to give Ollie a chance.

thirty seven

Frigliana, in southern Spain, is a quaint whitewashed village. Its narrow cobblestone streets, where all of the houses are tastefully decorated with colourful ceramic tiles and flowerpots and greenery adorn the pathways, have contributed to its acclaim for being one the 'Most Prettiest Villages' in Andalusia.

Esme had visited this area before. She'd chosen this place for their honeymoon because, in September, it was less touristy. She also wanted to show Alastair the local Archaeological Museum, which as well as being a piece of art in itself, also housed many pieces of art dating back to the Neolithic Age and up to the present day. She knew that he'd be interested in the contemporary art section.

After collecting their hire-car from Malaga airport, they took the 'Route of Sun and Wine', passing through some charming villages including Cómpeta, Canillas de Albaida, Torrox and Nerja, before ending up at their destination.

"We must make time to visit these places whilst we're here, Es."

"I've visited some of these places before, darling. They're brimming with beauty and culture."

"I can only imagine!"

The sat nav directed them to the main gates of a large white villa, where the owner was waiting for them outside.

Welcoming them in, Alastair drove under a wide covered archway and parked the car.

After showing them around and explaining the workings and the alarm system, he left them to enjoy a specially prepared lunch.

Sitting together on the wrap-around terrace, overlooking the pool and the magnificent landscape, they shared the same opinion that Frigliana was a spectacular place to be.

Perusing the many leaflets which the owner had kindly left for them, they were pleased to see that there weren't any large supermarkets or shopping outlets in the area and they understood why many artists and historians had made it their haven.

From reading the 5-star recommendations in one of the promotion leaflets, they decided to book a table at The Garden Restaurant for dinner.

Cooling down in the infinity pool, they finished their wine before snoozing in the afternoon sun.

Later that evening, after dining on fresh fish and vegetables, washed down with a bottle of Cava, they mingled with the villagers and other visitors who were strolling through the white labyrinth of houses and small shops; all of which were run by inhabitants of the village.

Esme cast her mind back to the last time she'd

visited Frigliana with her friend, when she'd bought a triangular shaped bracelet from a local silversmith. She noticed that he was still there, operating from the lower part of his home which he'd adeptly converted into his workshop.

"Well, this is really 'picture book', isn't it Es?"

Smiling, she bobbed her head.

"It really is! We have two glorious weeks to explore it and the surrounding areas. You're going to love it!"

Her mind wandered to the enjoyable times she'd spent on Burriana Beach with her friend who'd once lived in Nerja. She smiled as she remembered how they'd both struggled to walk uphill from the beach, after drinking several glasses of champagne.

They'd also trekked along the Chillar River Trail, with its scenic landscape and its free flowing waterfalls. She'd never forget that ethereal moment.

She just knew that Alastair would appreciate visiting those places, too!

Arm in arm, they meandered back to their rented villa, both acknowledging how very fortunate they were to be experiencing the grandeur and beauty of the historic village and its surroundings.

thirty eight

The following morning after breakfast, they decided to take an impromptu drive along the coast.

As he tuned the radio, the sound of an English DJ was announcing that he was going to play a medley of Stevie Wonder's songs. Almost immediately, he started to sing along.

"There's a place in the sun and before my life is done, got to find me a place in the sun."

Recalling how she'd bought an album of the Motown singer in 1969, she also sang along.

Looking up, she saw a large 'for sale' placard on the hillside.

"Alastair, could you just come off at the next turning. I've just seen something interesting."

He'd also spied it.

After leaving the road, they drove along several short lanes before they found the partly-constructed house. The plot was cordoned off with some block wooden fencing, but the upper part of the structure was visible.

"Well, this is a find, isn't it Es?"

Nodding, her pulse quickened.

Enthusiastically tapping the agent's number into his phone, he made an appointment to view the property.

"We can view it at 2.00 this afternoon. Let's look around the vicinity and see what it has to offer."

Chatting non-stop, they drove slowly around Cortija San Rafael, admiring the exclusive residential area with its 360-degree panoramic views of the mountains and the sea.

After eating lunch at a small family-owned café, they made their way back to the plot for their appointment.

As the agent opened the access gate and began his spiel, both hurried onto the land to explore.

"The owner is having personal issues which need to be resolved quickly and can't continue with the build."

Alastair pondered on whether the agent should be disclosing this information.

Casting glances at his wife, he asked numerous questions before discovering that if the house didn't sell within the next three days, the bank would firmly foreclose. Recently several unreasonable offers had been declined and the owner was willing to let the bank repossess it, rather than give it away for a stupid price.

"Can you arrange a meeting with the guy? I'd like to take a closer look at his drawings and find out more about the structure."

Whilst the agent was talking to the vendor, they continued to explore the half-built shell.

"What do you think, Es? Could you live here? It's a quiet area, isn't it? We could do so much with this. I can't wait to see the plans."

"I love it. Just look at those amazing views. It's spectacular. My mind is working overtime now, trying to envisage it when it's finished. I'd love to live in this part of Spain."

Squeezing his hand, she nestled into him.

"Let's see if we can do a deal, Es. I'll offer him a fair price. Let's see what he comes up with first."

The agent approached them.

"He can meet you here this evening at seven, if that's ok with you."

"Seven it is. We'll be here."

Returning to the villa, they couldn't contain their excitement. In their mind's eyes, they'd already completed the house build and could see themselves living in it.

"I really believe this will work for us, Alastair. We can make a new life here. It's the right time for us to do it."

"You know something, I believe it is. Even though I've never been here before, the place seems enigmatically familiar to me. It's like a déjà vu thing. I feel at home in this area."

Acknowledging his sense of familiarity and her own intuition, she believed that they were both a vibrational match and that their interests, their past experiences and their life purposes had attracted them to each other. Their conscious connection felt very comfortable and, it was perfectly feasible that their subconscious connection was historic.

****

At 7.00pm prompt, the owner approached them with a set of plans under his arm and a laptop, as they waited outside.

Dressed in smart casual attire, he introduced himself as Mateo.

Following a tour of the plot, he laid out the plans across a pile of building blocks.

Scrutinising every minute detail, Alastair was suitably impressed. Placing his glasses onto the edge of his nose, he glanced over at his wife.

Nodding in approval, she smiled.

With excitement escalating, he enquired about the price.

He'd discovered that some of the houses in the area could fetch up to three million euros and well above. Mateo would sell it to them for a million. He urgently needed to pay his ex-wife off as part of a hefty divorce settlement. She was 'taking him to the cleaners', after she'd caught him cheating on her with her best friend. It was easier to give her what she wanted, rather than drag it through the courts. She was to have their marital home and a shedload of money to go with it.

Alastair was eager to find out more about the property.

"Let's go to a local bar and we can discuss the deal further."

"Ok. Follow me."

Listening to him asking endless questions of critical importance, Esme again witnessed his Socrates persona.

After agreeing the mutually-beneficial deal, it was decided that Mateo would continue to supervise the build, using his own tradesmen and his existing suppliers; under Alastair's watchful eye, of course. He'd also provided them with the addresses of other residences which he'd constructed in the surrounding areas, so they could view the standard of his work.

Mateo would be a useful asset. He'd be able to sort out any occurring issues. He'd reassured them of his excellent standards and was grateful for having the opportunity to complete the build. His workmen could now return to work and earn a living.

His subtle strategy of offering a generous bonus for early completion, would also ensure that the dwelling would be completed within a matter of months.

As they left the bar, the newly-weds couldn't quite believe what they'd done. Within the space of less than twelve hours, they'd impulsively purchased a part-built property.

From looking at the plans, the house had a biophilic heavy aesthetic, like their own home and in the other recent structures that Alastair designed. Reducing carbon footprint and connecting their home with nature was important to them.

By mostly using the latest sustainable building materials and by incorporating natural and organic elements into the structure and garden areas, Mateo was way ahead of his game.

Spontaneity had dropped in on him again.

After his unexpected brush with death, it was a stark reminder of the importance of seizing the moment.

Now was definitely the time to grasp it. Squandering the opportunity wasn't an option! Carpe diem!

thirty nine

Over breakfast the following morning, they planned their route to visit several of the houses on Mateo's list.

Some dwellings were in the prestigious areas of Puerto Banus and Marbella. Others were in the equally impressive areas of Nerja and Torrox.

Suitably impressed with each of the exclusive structures, they stopped at a supermarket on the way home to buy some groceries and wine.

At lunchtime, they'd eaten a substantial platter, consisting of chunks of herb-crusted bread, oak-smoked salmon, Manchego cheese, deep fried squid, Marconi almonds, garlic-filled olives and fresh grapes. For dessert, they indulgently dipped and savoured several cinnamon-coated churros into a bowl of melted caramel sauce.

Following an afternoon nap, they decided to venture out for the evening. The friendly taxi driver chatted animatedly, recommending several bars, before reaching their drop-off point in Nerja.

Meandering through the narrow streets, filled with restaurants and shops selling leatherwear, clothing and jewellery, their ears guided them towards an Irish bar in Calle Carabeo which was belting out Irish ballads through the loud sound system. Nostalgia tugged at her heartstrings as she recalled Leo singing and performing an energetic jig to those songs.

After managing to squeeze through the crowded bar, they ordered two halves of Guinness and stood with a group of lively holidaymakers who were having fun, singing and dancing along to the tunes of a fiddle-playing musician.

Chatting to the group, they discovered that they hailed from Dublin and the bar was a regular haunt of theirs when they holidayed in Nerja.

The familiar lilt of their silken accent, with its elongated vowels, gave her goosebumps. As a man standing next to her, initiated a conversation, she shivered.

"What's the story, lass? A-ware-ya?"

Leo always used to ask her the same question.

"I'm grand", she replied.

Amused at her response, her husband smiled.

As the music resumed, one of the girls grabbed Esme's arm and attempted to drag her onto the dance floor. Without hesitation, she handed Alastair her bag and joined the three other girls who were already positioning themselves for the dance. As the audience clapped and tapped their feet along to the fast tempo, the quartet duly performed their impromptu jig.

Holding her torso rigid and her arms straight by her side, she raised her right foot up to her knee and hopped to the rhythm of the music; just like Leo had patiently taught her several years ago.

Proudly, Alastair's eyes never left her, as she struggled to keep up with the energetic pace of the youngsters as they hopped and pointed their feet.

Not possessing their stamina or their core strength, she was more than thankful when the music ended.

As they all left the dance floor, an eruption of applause and raucous laughter rang throughout the bar.

Nearly collapsing into his arms, she wondered why she had even joined in with the girls in the first place. Nevertheless, it had been an exhilarating experience.

On the way home in the taxi, he teased her.

"Well, you'll have no trouble sleeping tonight, will you?"

forty

After her lively performance the previous evening, the soles of her feet throbbed, her calves ached. She was still tired as she stepped out of bed.

Following a leisurely late breakfast, she idly relaxed by the pool, taking several dips to ease her sore muscles, whilst Alastair spoke with his solicitor.

Furnishing him with the particulars of the half-completed house and the name of Mateo's lawyer, he was more than eager to get things moving.

Even though searches hadn't been undertaken and contracts hadn't been signed, they'd already been collaborating their ideas and designs.

Escaping the midday sun, they sat at a large table under the shade of a white overhanging parasol, scrutinising the architectural drawings of their soon-to-be dwelling.

In the distance, she could see the North African coastline lying just beyond the shimmering Mediterranean.

Impressed with the attention to detail which had been given to the design of the house, he liked how the glass and concrete complemented each other and how the house had been strategically positioned to take in the spectacular views.

The skillful ease in which his pencil moved instinctively across the paper, as he sketched several unconventional designs of form and emptiness, fascinated her. She'd also been drafting ideas and had already started compiling her own mood board for different sections of the interior of the house.

Her deep understanding of the colour palette and appreciation of textures had originated even before she'd embarked on her studies at university. She'd successfully honed her skills by her completion of highly-acclaimed commissions since then.

"Shall we go and visit those caves in Nerja tomorrow, Es?"

"That would be nice. I think we can book it through their website. It'll save us queuing up."

Leaving him to continue with his sketching, she went inside to make the booking and prepare some tapas.

After lunching on Spanish omelette, some chilli prawns dipped in harissa mayonnaise and toasted bread drizzled with oil and finely chopped tomatoes, they relished the moment of unstructured routine beside the pool, as they slowly sipped several flutes of sparkling Cava.

She was so looking forward to embracing the simpler pleasures of nature and the dramatic sunsets from their terrace.

Whilst discussing the structural aesthetics of their newly-acquired home, he achingly held onto her every word as she enthused about how she'd like to design and sculpt something for the garden.

His eyes adoring every inch of her slender frame, she knew exactly what he was thinking. She was thinking the same. The sun and the wine always had this effect on her and, anyway, it was their honeymoon!

Slowly, she stood up and walked towards him, her glistening eyes revealing her desireful intentions.

Taking hold of his hand, she led him across the

177

garden and into the house, their bare soles embracing the coolness of the marble floor.

The energy-charged chemistry between them was palpable.

"It's my turn to show you something, Alastair."

forty one

Arising early, they ate a light breakfast. Their guided tour of the caves had been booked for 9.30.

After parking the car, they approached the entrance, where the tour guide along with several other eager visitors, were waiting for them.

Before entering the Nerja caves, they were shown a short audio-visual presentation of the history and were fascinated to learn that, over the centuries, the pre-historic caves had been used as a burial site, a habitat for numerous unique species of animals and a site for cultural expression.

Remnants, which included imprints of small invertebrates and pseudo-scorpions, were testimony that hunters and fishermen from over 30,000 years ago had once occupied the caves.

As they meandered around the caves, which is the home of the world's largest column of stalagmite and stalactite measuring 32m in height and 13.7m at its base, they were informed that it had retained its status in the Guinness World Records since 1989.

"Es. Just look at those red painted stalagmites. They're unbelievable!"

Totally engrossed in the spectacular natural beauty, she nodded.

The guide proceeded to explain that they'd likely been splattered or blown onto the rock by Neanderthals, who'd created the magnificent art. The mysterious symbols and codifications, which were displayed on the multiple formations, were deemed to have been caused by a massive earthquake .

Enlightened by other facets of antediluvian information, they listened intently, reluctant to leave when the guide hurriedly informed them that the short tour was reaching its end. They hadn't seen enough of this natural beauty.

Thrilled to hear that some private visits, allowing entrance to more of the underworld caves were available during the day and evenings, Alastair enthused.

"Let's get booked onto one of those tours, Es. We most definitely need a second visit here."

As they reached the entrance to the caves, they joined the queue at the booking office and placed a reservation for the night tour.

forty two

Following two eventful weeks on their honeymoon, they returned to England.

His first job to was to make sure everything was in hand for the official opening of Habitaire. He made the call. Everything was under control.

The residents had already occupied their rooms and had been involved in many educational activities. Alastair had been there to welcome them on their arrival and had joined in with some of their therapy sessions.

Since living in Spain, he'd taken to dressing more casually. It was important that his informal, yet smart attire and image fitted in with the relaxed culture and environment, if he was to reach out to the men.

Once each applicant had been assessed as having reached a level where they would be be able to function semi-independently, they would then be accepted onto the transitional programme, which would facilitate their progress onto the next period in their lives. The proviso being that they would sign a formal contract, which included the strict expectations of how they would promise to respect their accommodation and adhere to Habitaire's rules and regulations.

Being guaranteed at least a six month stay, they'd be encouraged to find voluntary work, stay dry and stay clean.

If they flouted the rules, they'd be given two

chances, but if they continued to violate them, they'd be asked to leave and a referral to another support group would then be completed. They just had to take responsibility for their actions.

All would be required to contribute part of their benefits in the form of paying a minimal rent, which would teach them how to efficiently manage their money and would subsidise the running costs of the premises.

All but two men were on medication and would receive their daily prescription from a volunteer medical practitioner, who'd closely monitor their behaviours and symptoms.

The fact had to be faced that the men were human and that there was a distinct possibility that they would relapse. Having been dependent for many years, it could take several attempts before they found their way out of their state of needing.

It was imperative that, during their low periods, they didn't resort to obtaining drugs from other sources, or using their benefits to buy alcohol. Their support workers would also closely monitor for any evidence.

Invitations to attend the opening had been sent to various organisations, who'd been involved since the project initiation phase up to the project execution and he was pleased to hear that all had confirmed that they'd be attending.

The list included the owner of the building, who continued with his offer of using his premises at zero cost and the construction firm's CEO and his employees, who maintained the premises; also at no cost.

Others on the invite list were the chairperson

of the city's homeless organization and a manager from the council's social housing department. Counsellors, benefit officers, representatives from two charities, support workers, a teacher from the local community centre, a volunteer medical practitioner and a library manager.

All members of the Steering Group were available to attend, as were Alastair and Esme's neighbours from Chancel Quarter, who had been involved from the start and had generously given their time, as well as various goods and monetary donations.

For the important event, Camellia and Stefano would provide the food and drinks. Obviously, no alcohol would be allowed on the premises. They'd continued with their promise to donate weekly food parcels of fresh fruit, vegetables, meat or fish and dairy products to the residents. Eating healthily had been factored into the recovery programme.

Nick and Trish had already provided each resident with a £150 donation, which had enabled them to buy new clothes for the event.

To further the residents' learning, Tina and Dave, would present the men with stationery items, including pens, jotters, journals and various genres of book. A local library had also donated a substantial number of books. The journals would assist them in keeping a daily log of their progress, as well as listing their successes, however small. They'd already been attending life skills classes and a creative writing course, which had seen an improvement in their mental health and physical well-being.

Not only was it important to recognise all the hard work that had been put in to bring the project to fruition, but it was also imperative that communication lines with members of the network remained open to ensure continued support.

Satisfied that all was in place for the event, all he had to do was prepare an outline of his speech and make some brief notes. He'd run it past Esme once he'd finished it.

forty three

Ready and waiting for the attendees to arrive, he welcomed each one with a smile and a handshake, mingling until everyone on the list had arrived. Proficient in the art of presentation, he'd already made an immediate connection.

"Good afternoon. As we've all met before, I don't need to introduce myself, but I will anyway. I'm Alastair."

An impromptu reply from one of the residents surprised him and he grinned cheerfully.

"Hiya Alastair, I'm Joe."

Ripples of laughter embraced the room.

"Firstly, I'd like to thank all of you who are involved in the project. Those of you who've taken those courageous first steps to a place of uncertainty, hoping to find some peace in your lives and all of those who've been involved in one way or another, in getting the project off the ground. You've been totally committed to meeting the deadline for the opening of Habitaire and for that, I'm so very grateful for your help."

Raising his hands high, he clapped loudly in appreciation and his audience returned his sentiments.

"Before I continue, I'd like to ask you to listen carefully to the powerful and heartfelt lyrics of a song which I'm now going to play for you. When you've heard it, maybe you'll understand why I chose it and why it is relevant to every human being in this room."

Pressing the remote, the first piano chords of

185

the song began playing.

Most of the audience, mainly the older ones, immediately recognised the song, some singing along to it, whilst others were silently mouthing the words.

Smiling, he scanned the space, making a mental note of the audience's reactions. They had 'locked in' immediately.

Allowing them a little time to absorb the lyrics, he glanced over towards the corner where his wife was standing. Her presence in the room and, her presence in his life, was constant fuel for his creativity. She inspired him.

The absence of any other noise emphasised the impact it had had on them. Some people were holding the palm of one hand over their mouths. Others were touching their eyes. Some cast sideways glances.

"I'm sure most of you will be familiar with the song, but for those of you who haven't heard it before, after being inspired by The Swan Silvertones, who were a gospel group, Bridge Over Troubled Water was written by an American singer, Paul Simon in 1969. A year later, he recorded and released the song with his singing partner, Art Garfunkel."

Smiling, the older members of the audience bobbed their heads several times in agreement.

"If you'll bear with me, I'd like to give you my own take on the song and how it touches me. If we examine the title, we can take three words out of it – bridge, troubled and water – and then later we can analyse how it fits in with where we are today."

From the expressions on the faces in front of him, he knew he'd hooked them and was already holding their attention.

"Let's look at the first word, bridge. A bridge is a support that needs to be strong to carry a heavy load. It must also be strong so that it doesn't bend under its own weight. It connects one community to another."

Ali was smiling. Although he understood a little of what was being said, he didn't understand most of it.

Alastair returned his smile before continuing.

"In relation to the intention of why this building has been purposely renovated for use, the bridge could represent the human connection between those who may be struggling and those who can be 'of service', to relieve the long-standing suffering of their fellow humans during their many periods of crises."

Unexpectedly, he felt his mouth go dry and he could feel a lump in his throat. Clearing his throat a few times, he swallowed, aware that his audience would have spotted his emotional connection with the subject matter.

"For me, I see the bridge as the crossing from one traumatic stage in someone's life to a better place when they reach the other side. So, for all those here today who have showed courage and were willing to cross over the bridge, not knowing what would await them on the other side, I salute you and wish you brighter days ahead."

He took a sip of water.

"Someone once told me that he felt the song was about God being the bridge over his troubled waters, especially when he felt he'd no one to guide him through his aching loneliness and the darkest moments in his life."

Murmuration in the audience alerted him to the possibility that some individuals hadn't agreed with what he'd just said. Without hesitation, he took control, swiftly addressing the issue.

"I'm not preaching to you. I'm only relaying someone's interpretation. Whatever you may believe in, be it God, Source, Buddha, the Universe or if you have humanistic beliefs, this man had found a spiritual connection in the song."

Stepping back, he amiably invited his audience to respond.

"Would any of you like to offer your views?"

A woman raised her hand and stood up.

"I would. With respect to what you just said about God, my view is that almost all religions are controlling. As children, we're indoctrinated with our parents' religious beliefs and norms. Unquestionably, we are taught what to think and what to believe, until we just accept it that what we're hearing is the truth. I think it's inappropriate. It can lead to children being indecisive and unable to form their own opinions. As we get older, our personal experiences form our own views and some of us will challenge our forced beliefs and then change our thinking."

From the corner of his eye, he noted that some of the residents were grinning, whilst others pressed their lips tightly.

"I'm a humanist. I have morals and I believe that every human is equal and should be treated with dignity. We're all unique and we all have a free will to choose what we want to believe."

He hadn't expected that the word 'God' would evoke such an emotional recall of memories.

Determined, she continued.

"Having had contact with the residents, I'm very optimistic that they all have the potential to overcome their painful childhood and adult episodes and that they have grown from their experiences. Whichever way society has mistreated them by ignoring their troubled waters, I've witnessed a positive change since I first met the group. They're learning to think for themselves and love themselves. I'm aware my beliefs may not bode well with those who have strong religious beliefs, but I just had to voice my feelings."

A man's voice interrupted.

"So, isn't humanism another organised belief system, then? There are many religions who hold the same views as your religion, even though you don't class it as a religion. Christians also believe in what you believe in. I, also have morals, agree that every human is unique, equal, has a free will and should be treated with dignity. I have a faith, believe in God and I'm respectful of other faiths and beliefs."

Intuitively, she knew that all eyes would be on her; some judging; some not.

"I politely accept what you say and I own what I think."

Unapologetically indicating her desire to decline any additional discussion, she sat down.

Whilst Esme appreciated her female resilience and her unflinching authentic resolve to speak out and challenge, she could also resonate with the man's point of view.

Alastair drank the dregs of water from his glass before refilling it. He'd welcomed the interaction. His voice needed a rest. Although the audience seemed to be enjoying the discussion, he needed to move one.

"Thank you for your views. I'm now going to ask Esme to give her thoughts on another word in the title, 'troubled'.

Striding confidently towards to the lectern, she stood behind it and adjusted the microphone.

"Hello everyone. I will keep it short. After hearing the lyrics and focusing on the word 'troubled', the first thing that came into my mind was a troubled soul who has lost their way and is unable to function in a way that is beneficial for their mental health and physical wellbeing. Other phrases and words which sprang to mind were, carrying a burden of buried memories, beset by anxiety, worry, misery, abuse and misfortune."

Recollections of the times she'd worked with women who'd faced domestic violence, had enabled her to bring the vocabulary to the forefront.

"From my experience of working with women who'd been made homeless and were fortunate enough to be rescued from the streets by a homeless charity, I have witnessed overpowering feelings of hopelessness and a lack of self-worth by fragile women who were frightened, confused and apprehensive of what the future held for them. Their persistent distress had changed their once-confident personalities and they felt that they were carrying the weight of the world on their shoulders. I think we can all relate to the word troubled, if we reflect on our own past experiences. Thank you for listening to me."

Amidst the applause, she bowed her head and walked slowly back towards her seat.

"Thank you, Esme. May I now ask the owner of this building, Mr Hoffman, for his views on the word 'water'."

A tall upright gentleman in an expensive-looking suit made his way forward. His outward appearance did not match his inner character. Far from it! His genuine understanding and generosity towards this diverse group of men had already made a massive difference to their lives.

"Good afternoon. When Alastair asked me to analyse the word 'water' in the title, I scribbled lots of notes. So, I'll make use of those notes now."

From a sheet of A4 lined paper, he referred to bullet points as he began his own assessment.

"Water is infinite. Without water, human life would cease to exist. In fact, it's been said that water is the source of life itself and that it holds endless inspiration and knowledge. Taoists believe that water symbolises transformation and wisdom. It doesn't resist anything in its way. It just flows. They also believe that if blocked by any solid object, water finds its way around it and goes where it want to go. Water is a dominant force. It's persistent ebb and flow of the ocean is powerful enough to wear away any piece of hard rock"

His voice, firm and well-balanced, was pitch-perfect. Some raising of eyebrows and rolling of eyes from several listeners, didn't go unnoticed as Alastair gauged their reactions.

"Water can be mysterious in that we don't really know what is happening beneath its surface. Similar to the way in which we don't know what is happening under the surface of humans, we don't know how they feel. How can we know if they don't tell us? For whatever reason, they may not feel able to reveal their feelings."

Esme reflected on the time her husband was

wading through his own troubled water after the attack and resonated with his noteworthy narrative.

"Water washes away any dirt. When we rinse it over our bodies, it cleanses us. When we drink it, it has a cleansing effect on our system. When we swim in it, it energises us and keeps us healthy. Water is flexible and it can teach us to be flexible also. By finding ways around those obstacles in our lives and being less rigid, we can refuse to stand still and make making changes that will benefit us."

Projecting his voice and shifting his gaze to several individuals, he continued to paint the picture.

"Finally, different cultures around the world regard water as being sacred and a symbol of renewal."

Presuming he'd finished speaking, Alastair moved forward.

"Can I just finish by saying that I really got a lot out of completing this task. It made me realise the many times I have resisted change in my life and the many opportunities that I have missed by being inflexible. Thank you, Alastair. I intend to start making some changes in my life."

"That's good to hear, Mr Hoffman. I appreciate your input."

A loud round of applause indicated that he'd captured the mindsets of his listeners.

"Well, I think it's time to take a break. If you want to make your way over to the kitchen area, you'll find some refreshments. I'll join you in a moment."

Realising that the first half may have been a bit heavy going for some, he justified the content to himself. It slotted in with the key purpose of what Habitaire represented. To house and rehabilitate the

192

homeless.

As he approached the others, he sensed that the message hadn't fallen on deaf ears. From the buzzing conversations, it was positive proof that some listening and reflection had taken place.

forty four

During the interval, Esme had also before been subtly intermingling, eavesdropping on the conversations between the residents and the guests.

It quickly became apparent that Alastair's intended use of the three words to encourage his audience to relate song to situation, had ignited several unexpected extras. For some, it had brought back pleasing memories of younger days, without even registering the key message that the lyrics portrayed. For others, it had obviously released buried emotions, as they freely unlocked their own adversities and divulged how they hadn't dealt with the residue.

Thinking of how some deep wounds are not visible to the human eye, she watched as the residents returned to their seats, all looking smart in their new attire. Some shuffled in their seats and fidgeted, whilst others flicked their hair and adjusted their clothing.

At the start of the second half of the event, he explained that the men would be giving accounts of their personal feelings and thoughts about living in Habitaire, before relaying what had prompted him to persuade others to become involved in the opening of the safe and secure accommodation.

"Going back to the song, 'when you're down and out, when you're on the street, reminds me of the first time I saw Ali. By the way, he's given me permission to say this. It was raining heavily when I first saw him. He was sitting in a doorway near my place of work, shivering with a threadbare blanket

194

around his shoulders to keep him warm. His worldly possessions were in two plastic bags at the side of him."

Alastair looked at Ali and smiled reassuringly.

"On my return to the office, I stopped to chat and handed him a sandwich and a hot drink. I discovered that Ali was a legal refugee from Syria. On arrival here, he'd lived with his cousin and, after a disagreement, he'd been asked to leave. Without any place to go, he ended up on the streets."

Turning around, he caught Ali's eye and tilted his head.

"It's hard to explain what I felt at the time. Guilt for not having noticed him before and, for him being deprived and homeless, whilst I enjoyed a comfortable lifestyle. Guilt for my own ignorant assumptions and my wrong judgements. Guilt for not recognising the many variables of the unavoidable situations that homeless people find themselves in. Guilt for compromising my own moral standards and not doing something sooner to help those who are less fortunate than me."

He paused for a moment to let his honesty filter throughout the room.

"Ali was the trigger that made me commit to doing something to help the homeless in the city. That is when I approached some friends and business acquaintances to get involved. You know, in an ideal world, we'd all have a roof over our heads, food in our bellies and people who care about us, but widespread disillusionment in a society which doesn't respect the basic rights of our fellow humans, unfortunately still exists."

Waving his hand, he signalled Ali to join him.

"Do you have something to tell us?"

"Yes, Ali Sir. I speak now."

He'd been practicing his speech all week and was proud to be speaking in front of everyone.

Alastair touched his arm and stood close.

"I come from Syria to England one year back. It wasn't good. Bad conflict there. I lived with cousin, but he didn't want me to stay, so I lived on streets. No money. No job. Ali Sir helped me. I live in here now. The English people are good to me. I'm warm and feel safe. No crying. Sorry, my English not good. Sorry. I learn."

Despite his fractured attempt at speaking the English language, everyone seemed enamoured by his humble confidence and moved by the way in which he'd politely addressed Alastair as Ali Sir.

Slightly embarrassed by the loud applause, he bowed humbly in appreciation, before being handed the box of gifted stationery.

Contemplating on the discernable contrast between where he'd been living only a few months ago, to where he was living now, Esme deliberated on how daunting it must have been for Ali to initially integrate into a different culture and equally as scary to be left homeless and alone, forsaken by someone he'd trusted.

"Thank you, Ali. Let's hear from David now."

An energetic clapping of hands escorted him back to his seat.

Anxious to get his ordeal over with, the next speaker sidled up next to Alastair and rapidly delivered his rehearsed speech.

"Hello. This is a great place to live. Compared with where I've lived before, it's a palace. I feel secure here. We all do. It's good that I have a postal address and there's someone on reception all the time. The door is locked and no one can get in. See them over there, they're my family. Hey, guess what? I think I might have a job in the café next door. It's just washing dishes, cleaning tables and the floor. They said that they'd let me know on Monday. Keep your fingers crossed that I get it. I hope I do. Oh! Thanks for listening to me. Joe's next. Come on, it's your turn now."

Hearing the applause, he collected his gift box and bowed.

"Hiya, everyone. As he said, I'm Joe. I've only been here for a few weeks and I'm settling in nicely. I have my own room, my own key and I'm getting used to living a life of luxury. I'm still on medication and I'm staying dry. Not saying it's easy, it's fuc…. hard, man. Sorry, I nearly swore then. I have nothing but praise for all these people who look after us. Yeah. They understand us all. I'm so glad they gave me a place here and trusted me. I won't let you down, Mr Brickman. Promise you. I mean it, you know. I won't."

Inhaling deeply several times, Alastair was more than thankful for the loud handclapping.

"I know you won't, Joe. Here, this is for you."

"Thanks. I forgot to introduce Phil."

As Phil walked towards him, they fist-bumped each other.

"Hi everyone. I'm a bit nervous, so if I start to stutter, please forgive me. I want to say a massive thank you to the people who've let me come to live here.

I'm so grateful that they believed in me. I have good days and bad days, but there's always someone to talk to about my problems. Me and the others have a cup of tea and some biscuits and sometimes we talk a load of shite. Sorry, I mean rubbish and we have a great laugh. At least we get it off our chests, don't we lads? We're here for each other."

Laughing loudly, they raised their thumbs.

"We go to some great sessions in the Learning Room. There's a lady over there, I won't tell you her name, who comes in to do some creative play with us. Now, I know you might think that sounds childish, but she told us that we are exploring our inner child and discovering ourselves."

Totally aware that the audience would be intrigued by what Phil had just declared, the woman who'd voiced her opinion about religion earlier waved at him. The cathartic sessions had released some of the men's buried childhood memories and unfulfilled emotional needs.

Not only had the men shared their inner experiences with each other, they'd also put pen to paper for the first time in a long time; all evidence that they were now doing something that they'd been afraid to do. Trusting in the unseen, they'd stepped outside of their past and taken that first step into the unknown.

"So, last week, me and David built a row of Lego houses. They were a bit like the row of terraced houses in different colours, like the ones we used to live in as kids. It was so relaxing. We used to love Lego. Joe was sculpting figures out of modelling clay. They were dead good. He's a fantastic artist. He'd made his own little family. A mum, a dad and three kids in different sizes. I told him he could start his own business selling them. Didn't I, Joe?"

"Thanks for that, mate. You did."

"Ali did a fab drawing of the place where he used to live in Syria. He drew a pencil drawing of the block of flats he used to live in before they were bombed out. I watched him as he drew lots of straight and scribbly lines. Then he used his fingers to blend it all in. He said it was easy. I don't think I could draw like that."

Ali waved and smiled.

"Hey, Mr Brickman. Is it ok if I carry on talking here? I said I was nervous. I can't shut up, can I?"

His dry sense of humour and openness had the listeners hooting with laughter.

"Carry on, Phil. We're all enjoying it."

"Ok then. I'll just tell you what Danny and Ian did. I don't know how I'm remembering all this. I'm usually quite forgetful. Let me think. Yeah. I've got it now. They did some mandalas. Shall I tell you what a mandala is? It's just a circle really. It has its own meaning when you do it yourself. Theirs were just simple ones with a circle in the middle with ten triangles around it. A bit like pieces of a pie. Whilst David was finishing drawing his houses, I was spying on them. They did a drawing of themselves in the middle and then they did smaller drawing of the things they remembered when they were kids in the triangles. I want to do one of them next time."

His comedic banter produced more laughter.

"Oh! Have I forgot anybody? I have. It's Billy. He painted a great picture of a dream he kept having when he was a kid. He still has those dreams now. It was a bit weird really. Sorry for saying that, mate. I didn't get it."

"Oh! I get it, Phil. I've been bloody dreaming it

for twenty odd years. I know exactly what it's about."

"You'll have to tell me more about it then, won't you? Tell me next week when we're on our own. Hey, I'd better shut up and give someone else a chance. Ian, come on, it's your turn ."

As Ian left his seat, he began talking again.

"I've forgot to tell you something else, as well. We're only going to be having philosophy discussions over the next few weeks. We're going to talk about our relationship with ourselves and the world. Never heard of the word. She says it's so we can learn to develop our own voices. I'll shut up now. Honest!"

This guy was undoubtedly 'something else'. The audience loved him. Resounding laughter erupted and, as they enthusiastically clapped out his engaging performance, he gave an exaggerated bow.

"Hey, I nearly forgot my gift then."

Picking up the box, he grinned at his friend.

"Hiya. As he sed, me name's Ian. Before I came 'ere, I'd reached rock bottom. Me 'ed was dun in from the drugs and the ale. I was in another place before 'ere. It took 'em ages to get me sorted, but they dun a good job on me so I could come 'ere. I'm not sayin I'm proper sorted now, cuz I'm not, but I'm gerrin there, slowly, ya know. I takes me meds and does as I'm told. Sometimes, I feel as if I'm like a baby learning to walk. I fall down and then I get back up again, until I'm strong enough to take a few more steps."

Losing his balance, he began to shake. Alastair swiftly moved closer to steady him. Transferring his own energy into him, Alastair placed a firm hand on his back.

After a perpetual battle with his addictions, he'd accepted his body would need to gradually adapt to the changes.

"Take your time, Ian. You're doing ok."

"Sorry about that then. I went a bit dizzy. Da ya know that line in the song when it sez, 'sail on silver girl, well, some guy I knew used to sing it to us all and he sed that it was about a needle which was used to inject 'eroin, but that Paul Simon guy sed it was cuz his wife's hair was goin grey early when he wrote the song. Don't wan yer thinkin I'm goin all spiritual when I say this now, but do ya think that 'troubled water' means that the water is pushin us forward. What da ya think, Joe?"

"You could be right there, mate. We're defo moving."

"Come on, Danny. You're up next. Just wanna thank ya all for listenin to me prattlin. Appreciate it."

Exhausted, he unsteadily walked back to his seat clutching his gift, as the audience cheered and clapped.

"Hello everyone. I'll just say it as it is. Before I came here, I'd been in the same place as Ian. I felt as if I had no future. Didn't know where I'd end up. Well, I've been given another chance and I'm going to make the most of it. I'll keep shoving those dark clouds away and just do my best. That's all I can do, isn't it? By the way, this place is the best gaff I've lived in. So grateful for being here. Come on, Billy. You're next. Thank you for listening to me."

The clapping continued, as he collected his gift and fist bumped Billy on the way.

"Thanks, Danny. It's been a long time waiting over there for you lot to finish."

His friends cheered enthusiastically as they rummaged through the items in their boxes.

201

"In the other place, I had to work hard to show them that I meant what I'd said I'd do. It was tough going and I don't know how I did it, but I did. I had to do it, or I'd have ended up in the cemetery. I love it here. It's a safe place to live. I'm so thankful they believed in me and let me come here. You don't know what it means to me, Mr Brickman, to know that someone is willing to put their trust in you, like you've done with me. You listened and were so patient with me, as I unburdened my soul."

He'd been a high-flying executive, embracing uncertainty, taking risks, making instant decisions, until his unhealthy addictions which he'd used to control his exhausting mental burnout, had rapidly dominated his life. His successful career had been wrecked and most of his personal relationships had been destroyed. He was looking forward to attending the philosophy sessions and rediscovering himself.

Esme could hardly bear to watch, as her husband blinked rapidly and whilst pinching the bridge of his nose, he attempted to sniff discreetly. A solid lump surfaced in her throat and threatened to cut off her airways as she tried to focus on her breathing. He was displaying further signs of his emotional growth and, as his own vulnerability trickled down his cheeks, he indiscreetly wiped them away with his forefinger.

"It's good for my brain to be functioning again. I've already read quite a few of the fiction books from our library section. Going to see if I can get some other non-fiction genres from the charity shop. I want to find a job and get myself back into work."

Turning towards Alastair, he smiled.

"Thank you for directing me to those distance learning courses. I have already signed up and I'm working through them."

The audience started clapping and a man's voice could be heard over the noise.

"Good luck, Billy. Good luck."

"Just want to finish by saying a big thank you to everyone who's been involved in helping me to get a place in here and looking after me. I crossed the bridge and guess who I met on the other side. Those great guys over there. It's as if we were all meant to meet. Thank you to everyone here today for listening to me. I do appreciate it. Can I just say something else?"

Alastair nodded.

"I've learnt so much over this last year about how we tend to measure success by how much we earn and how rich some of us are. I used to think that way, but not anymore! Society rates the talented and the highly educated as being on a different level to those non-academics who are skilled in different areas. I've realised that everyone's search for success is different and that learning takes place in everything we do in our lives, not only in schools and universities. Intelligence comes in many forms and academia is not necessarily 'the be all and end all'. We need all kinds of different skills in this world of ours. Every human life on earth is important. We should be embracing that difference and we should surely be measuring success appropriately."

Pausing for a moment, he glanced over at his friends and winked reassuringly.

"Success, for us guys who've been to hell and back, has been nurturing our physical and mental health back to a state where we're beginning to function at a fairly reasonable level again. I think we've all now finally realised that our happiness lies within us."

He bowed his head and, whilst the audience's earsplitting applause continued, Alastair thought of how Billy's eloquent admission and his poignant explanation of his own perspective of success was thoughtworthy. Yes, success is relative. No one can judge what is a success or an achievement for another person. Only that person knows!

After handing him his gift box, Alastair cleared his throat several times and raised his eyes towards the ceiling before recapping.

The men's shared understanding of their own adversities and their mutual humane and healing love for each other, had emotionally taxed him. He'd absorbed so much from this event.

"Before we finish, I'll leave you to find your own meaning to the song. It can mean whatever you want it to mean. Interpret it in your own way. For me, it's a timeless communication that we can all take forward. For everyone here today, who has struggled to swim through their own troubled waters and, for those you are still struggling, my greatest wish for you is that you never lose hope. Hope will give you the strength and courage to ride those unexpected tidal waves."

He caught her staring at him and intimately possessed her stare for several moments.

Her already-quickened heartbeats intensified, further deepening their strong connection. Witnessing the close bond he'd formed with those brave men today, had served to confirm just one of the many reasons why she totally loved, respected and admired her protective husband. Once more, she'd seen inside his gentle and compassionate soul. She wondered if he knew how impactful his nurturing presence was having on their lives. His understanding of their needs had given them the strength to move forward and make changes in their lives. She could clearly see the impact the men were having on his life.

"It's been a privilege to be in your company today. Thank you once again for being involved. I wish you all a safe journey home. Good evening."

As he walked towards her, she thought of how society's expectations and the recognition of the rich 'privileged' achievers was viewed differently to the poor 'disadvantaged' achievers.

It was logical that the rich people who'd been born into money would have a different mindset. They believe being rich is a right. They'd see money as an opportunity and take risks to make even more money. They take it for granted, until they lose it.

It was equally rational to understand how the poor would also adopt a different mindset. Tending to settle for the steady approach, they think that being rich is a privilege. They see money as something to be earned; much like she had when she was younger and she still did to some degree. Both inclinations could be viewed as learnt behaviour.

Discerning that being rich wasn't necessarily bad or good. She thought it also depended on the individual's attitude towards having money or not. Although, she was equally conscious that not having enough to live on, could be very stressful.

Throughout her childhood and adult years, the same inequality had been directed at her. It was only later in life, when she'd become more self-actuated, that she began to recognise the necessity of conflicting opposites.

By treading a different path to the masses, her own success and spiritual growth had been achieved by not adhering to society's expectations.

forty five

Following the success of Habitaire, Mr Hoffman had made a spontaneous decision to renovate another part of the building to house vulnerable women.

Involvement in the homeless project had given him a renewed sense of purpose and had enhanced his life in many respects. It had allowed him to channel his energy into doing something that would help people to make changes in their lives.

Having hailed from a humble yet happy family, he could easily identify with poverty, but he'd never experienced not having a roof over his head.

His earlier lacking of luxuries had been his motivator to succeed in life. However, there'd been many a time when he'd realised that social mobility and money doesn't necessarily bring happiness or peace of mind.

He'd made more than enough money and had bought far too many properties in his life. With only his son to leave his fortune to, who also had more than enough, he wanted those in need to benefit from his years of hard work and success.

His involvement in Habitaire had made him a much happier person and far richer for doing so, though not in a monetary sense.

It was only after the opening event, when he'd delivered his views on the song, that there had been a serious awakening. He'd realised that he'd only been swimming at half capacity through his own troubled waters. He wanted to swim proficiently!

His wife had died ten years previously and, in his effort to cope with his grieving, he'd become insular.

Now, he was more spiritually connected and more attune with his inner self. He'd become aware of his own personal needs and his emotions. He had more energy and felt less isolated. Through meeting new people, his priorities were different.

A meeting of the Steering Committee had been arranged and he put forward his proposal.

All individuals involved in the conception of Habitaire had agreed to contribute in the same way as they had before.

The same purposeful business model would be used, the same structural design would be adopted and they'd strive to achieve the same duration of timescales for completion.

It was imperative that they opened it as soon as possible. Whilst the city was working flat out to tackle the problem, he knew more needed to be to done.

Within the self-same meeting, he'd mooted the idea of renovating the remaining part of the building for homeless families. He couldn't bear to think of children sleeping out rough on the streets. He'd also guaranteed, that as soon as the renovations had been completed and they'd received charitable status, he'd donate the entire premises and sign off the official documents.

Alastair had been the influencer who'd initially brought the idea of Habitaire to him. By using his expertise in business and his extensive knowledge of architecture and design, he'd easily been persuaded, along with many other professionals to join in with his quest to, not only alter society's view of homelessness, but to give some hope, support and love to the disadvantaged and vulnerable.

An intrinsic influencer of sorts in his early and teenage years, Alastair had been able to motivate his brother and his friends to take risks. Exploring endless possibilities, they'd not only had bundles of fun, but they'd learnt many life skills in the process.

He'd continued in this vein throughout his adult life, inspiring others to do their best and learn as much as they could, unrelentingly leading by his own example.

Always an independent maverick of sorts, it hadn't deterred him from being self-directed and highly ambitious as he forged ahead, following his own unique path – despite countless obstacles hindering his journey.

Endless external and internal sources had been his own motivators.

He'd strive for something and, once achieved, he'd be rewarded with praise, prizes and promotion. He'd used this exact method with his employees. What would be the point of striving to reach the end goal, if there wasn't some sort of reward at the end of it; be it kudos, money or just knowing that you'd done your best?

Each achievement had fuelled his creativity and drive. He'd always competed with himself, to exceed his own expectations and others' expectations of him too; not to boast, but to illustrate what could be achieved by not being scared to challenge cultural norms.

His critics had declared his extrinsic approach as lacking in purposefulness and meaningfulness and was difficult to maintain. Meaningful and purposeful in whose opinion?

He'd learnt that difficulties were presented to him for the purpose of his own growth; be it from an educational or spiritual perspective. It had taken as long as it took for him to succeed.

Intrinsically, his work in both a voluntary and paid capacity, had always been aligned with his values and the personal satisfaction it gave him when he knew he'd done a good job; especially when others had benefitted from his experiences and taken their own leaps of faith. Never once had he felt guilty when he was accused of 'rocking the boat' by being a non-conformer. His innovative and unconventional visions had spurned others to enhance their own lives by adopting his values and principles. Constantly and consistently, he'd helped them on their way to seeing that, with determination and insightful 'out of the box' thinking, they could also invest in their own expressive feelings of being the designer and the achiever of their own dreams.

Yes, Mr Hoffman had often silently and openly thanked Alastair Brickman for inviting him to become involved!

forty six

Alastair returned to Spain without Esme. There was house business to attend to and she had some small outstanding commissions to honour.

Aiming to complete the construction before she arrived in a few weeks' time, he was overawed to be met with a hive of activity as he entered the site.

On close inspection, he was more than pleased that the underfloor heating had been completed on time, which had then permitted the pale grey marble floor tiles to be laid throughout the ground floor level.

Standing back, he admired the full-height glass foyer and the spectacular wrap-around glazing of the contemporary structure, which allowed plenteous light to enter the immense internal space where clean lines dominated.

Landscape gardeners were diligently planting trees and numerous fragrant bushes in the already-established extensive grounds, which had been part of a sizeable acreage previously belonging to the neighbouring landowner.

Nodding his appreciation, as he continued to scrutinise, he observed numerous men meticulously perfecting the location of a tall Pheonix Palm tree, before embedding it firmly into the centre of the south-facing sun terrace which pleasantly overlooked the recently-installed infinity pool.

He was particularly impressed with the double width swivel door which he'd designed to enhance the entrance and to replace a heavy dark wooden door which had been on the original plans.

Clicking the remote, the door opened slowly to reveal stark white walls, which would serve as an ideal backdrop for the massive abstract paintings which Esme had commissioned from a young local artist.

The basement garage and gym were finished, as was the expansive driveway and the bio-dynamic lighting system.

Mateo had been true to his word and much had been completed since his last Zoom conversation and tour of the house. All jobs were on schedule for the completion date.

Satisfied with the swift progress, he drove to the villa, where they'd stayed for their honeymoon only a few weeks ago. Fortunately, he'd been able to rent it for an indefinite period until contracts were exchanged.

Most mornings, whilst on his early morning run, he'd ardently connect with the tweeting birds, the peaceful nature and grandiose landscape, inhaling the pungent aromatic herbs and floral wild scents. Exercise had always played an important part in his life. Not only did it retain his trim physique, it was also greatly beneficial for his mental health and his thought processing.

One particular morning, as he'd been sprinting along the undulating tracks with their steep slopes, his feet had slipped on the dusty gravel and he'd only just managed to save himself from falling into a deep ravine by gripping tightly onto an overhanging tree branch. The incident had taken him back to when he was a whippersnapper and a similar experience. Whilst clambering to his feet, he'd felt his mother's presence and clearly heard her tender voice, "Alastair, please be careful, son."

Oftentimes, he thought of her and the traumas she'd endured in her life.

When not meeting up with various suppliers and tradespeople, he would phone his friends and associates in England to monitor the progress at Habitaire. A Celebration of Achievements ceremony was in the planning stage for the men who'd attended various courses as part of their rehabilitation.

After wandering around the winding streets in the village, he'd popped into a small family restaurant for a bite to eat. He and Esme had eaten there several times and they'd been inspired to create the owner's home-made cuisine in their own kitchen.

He'd just finished eating when his phone rang.

Pressing the accept button, he smiled as he heard a familiar voice.

"Hello Ali Sir. How are you?"

"Hello Ali. I'm good thanks and you?"

"Yes. Alright, thanks. A quick call. I got new job at Habitaire."

"Excellent news."

Alastair had been coaching Ali on what to say in his interview and was already aware of his news. Without Ali's knowledge, he'd been instrumental in his friend being accepted for the position and had also provided a glowing reference.

To top up his earnings, Ali was working as an evening waiter in a restaurant whilst studying, as well as volunteering at the men's refuge where he'd previously lived. Although never being dependent on drugs and alcohol, his traumatic lived experience of homelessness and being amongst those who were, had enabled him to empathise and connect with the

213

others.

In his own country, he'd been working as a family support worker, but he hadn't gained any qualifications. He wanted to work with adults in a social setting, but his standard of English speaking, reading and writing wasn't high enough. Hence the reason for him attending college.

Ali was so excited. As well as supporting the residents, he'd also be some doing outreach work on the streets with different teams of qualified social workers.

He knew what he wanted out of his life, where he wanted to be - and he was willing to work hard to get there.

"Yer said if I believed in meself, things would get better. They did. I believed. I sing the song every day. You were me bridge over troubled water. You eased me mind and me time has come to shine."

Ali had touched his heart. He felt he'd been a father figure to him. Noticing that his friend's spoken English was improving, he smiled. He'd also acquired the local dialect.

"When I first meet you, I no understand my way. Now, I do!"

"Are you liking your studies, Ali?"

Alastair had always believed that education is the doorway to success and that you can never be overeducated.

"I'm liking it. It's boss."

"Any other news?"

"I speak to Ollie. He has more therapy and they let him to see his daughter. He says sorry for what he did to you."

The same message was repeated during each

of their conversations.

"I go now. I ring you Ali Sir and tell you how I am. Have good day. Tara."

After ending the call, he strolled back to the villa, reflecting on the most recent changes and decisive moments in his life.

His heartache, when his marriage to Jen had ended, had facilitated that first shift. Although she'd betrayed him, he'd accepted some responsibility.

Totally engrossed in his work, he'd neglected her needs and was oblivious to the obvious fractures in the relationship. He'd also forgiven her and he'd forgiven himself too.

In choosing to help Ali, he'd made a conscious decision to help others also, by collaborating with his friends to bring about change in their lives.

He'd found new love and married again. With Esme, he'd been willing to risk giving his heart away again. He needed her love. Wanting to spend the rest of his life with her felt natural.

He'd been stabbed. Whilst most would have perceived it as being a negative event, something positive had come out of it. The attack had forced him to make another significant decision; a decision which would take him through to the next stage in his life - retirement.

Alastair's personal reaction, by not wanting to prosecute, had provoked Ollie into considering how his addictions were affecting his life. He'd decided to do something about it.

Looking at the raised scar on his arm, he saw how quickly it was fading and flattening. Although it would always be visible, it was a significant reminder of the time he'd faced his inner turmoil and how he'd forgiven himself for not being there when members of his close family had died. More profoundly, it held memories of words which were spoken before his attack, "What would you fuckin know?" Words which now lay deeply embedded within his subconscious, surfacing every now and then to say hello.

He'd sold his business along with his brand name and his home.

Esme had also sold her rental properties and they'd, spontaneously, bought a new residence in a different country.

Contemplating on the feasibility of bizarre things happening for beneficial reasons, he was at peace with himself.

He felt as if he'd taken on a new identity. He had!

forty seven

The day had been productive in many aspects. Several teams of tradespeople were milling around the site, completing jobs from a precise snagging list.

He had spent most of the day with Mateo, inspecting and overseeing the completion of his new home.

During the afternoon, he'd taken time out to receive a pre-arranged telephone call from Ollie and his support worker.

When a vacant place had become available in Habitaire, Alastair had been instrumental in agreeing to a pilot project to see whether Ollie, at his current stage of recovery, could comfortably cope living in an independent environment.

He'd been pleased to hear that his plan was working and that Ollie was striving to remain clean and dry, no matter how tough it was, in the hope of gaining custody of his daughter in the future. She was his motivator!

On ending the call, he'd immediately received another call from Ali, updating him on his own progress.

After securing the site, he'd strolled back to the rented villa, contemplating on how he was looking forward to the following day and the beginning of yet another new chapter in his life.

He'd felt that he and Esme had achieved a balance. They were ready to enjoy the fruits of their labour and they'd enjoy sharing those fruits with others too!

forty eight

Arriving on the early morning flight from Manchester, Esme arrived just in time for their appointment to sign the relevant documents for their new house.

He had recently checked off all items on his snagging list with Mateo and was satisfied with the high standard of work which had been undertaken. As previously promised, a separate bonus was paid for the early completion.

She couldn't wait to get inside and start dressing each of the rooms. There wasn't that much to do really. Having previously liaised with the furniture and soft furnishing suppliers, along with the expert eye of her husband, all items had been delivered and were ready to be positioned within the fluid light-filled space.

The two commissioned pieces of artwork were waiting to be revealed and, as she carefully removed the packing, she was thrilled when she saw the way in which the artist had transferred her vision of sunshine yellow, bright red and cobalt blue into his design. The vertical and horizontal blurred lines of paint depicted the simple and sharp line lines of their unique home.

Almost immediately, she knew the precise position on the walls they would adorn.

Accompanied by her husband, she slowly surveyed every metre of the bare open space, free from ornate accents, on the ground floor before moving up the marble staircase to the equally naked middle and upper levels.

The middle level consisted of three large en-suite bedrooms, all having open views of the coast or the countryside.

Their perfectly proportioned sleeping area, situated on the uppermost level, afforded a visually appealing view of the coast. In the mirrors of her mind, she'd already envisaged the way in which she'd transform this space into a tranquil zone.

The sophisticated alarm system alerted them to a car which was parked outside the entrance to their property.

Alastair had arranged for two workmen who'd worked on the house, to move the stored seating and bedroom furniture from the garage into the house.

His voice activated the opening of the gates, allowing them to enter.

As all of the storage areas were discreetly enclosed within the internal structure, it was a simple task to position the functional, white leather seating into its chosen place.

By deliberately incorporating the use of subtle shades of white and pale greys with the vivid colours in their new pieces of geometric art, they'd introduced various textures and patterns to complement their aesthetic appreciation of minimalistic design.

Esme yawned. Her day had begun at 3.00am when her alarm went off. Issues at the airport caused her stress and she'd thought she may miss her flight. All in all, it had been an exhausting yet eventful day.

On their return to their rented villa, she ate a small platter of cheese and olives before flopping into bed and dreaming of how they'd enjoy including the finishing touches to their new abode.

forty nine

Before handing over the keys to the owner of the rented villa, they spent the next few days preparing the rooms for when they moved in.

Once installed in their peaceful sanctuary, it seemed as if their lives had taken on a new meaning. Away from the fast pace of their working lives, they enjoyed learning more about each other and the Spanish culture.

On several occasions, Esme had heard Alastair whistling and singing whilst he'd been pottering in the garden; all signs of his road to recovery.

More than content with their chosen lifestyle, they planned and cooked meals together, strolled lazily through the countryside near their home and ventured further into the most southerly region by car, exploring several historical places of interest.

They'd discovered that all of the whitewashed villages in and around Andalusia were constructed to defend the communities during conflicts and how the residents would preserve their traditional heritage by socialising and dining al fresco in the streets during the evenings.

One Saturday, they'd visited the morning market in Cómpeta, where they bought some sweet white wine which the locals had recommended and some fresh fish.

Mateo had kindly introduced them to some of his friends, who'd invited them to impromptu meals and local events.

Free from their constraints of established routines and early rising, they'd easily slotted into their new regime.

It was also nice to be dressed casually, instead of wearing business attire.

One morning, whilst her husband was out on his morning run, thoughts of Leo entered her mind. His face still visited her waking and sleeping dreams and his shadow sometimes unexpectedly appeared to reassure her. Never once did she imagine that she'd find anyone who could match up to him, until she met Alastair. Admittedly, after their first few dates, she did make comparisons. On analysis, they both possessed similar qualities. Both were gentlemen with a quirky sense of humour. Both were work-driven, both were generous souls and both were forgiving.

After preparing a generous platter of thinly sliced tomatoes drizzled with a blend of olive oil and fig balsamic vinegar, she topped them with some finely chopped shallots, green olives, basil leaves and several slivers of Manchego cheese. Dipping chunks of fresh baguette into the salad dressing, they leisurely ate their palatable lunch around the pool, whilst casually enlightening each other about earlier moments in their lives.

Extremely interested in her reminiscences, he admired how his wife spoke fondly and openly about her first husband and how his business had taken them to different countries. He was sure she'd mentioned it when they'd first met, but he allowed her to repeat the story. He'd probably repeated himself many times during their conversations. Maybe it was an age-thing!

Unperturbed, when she'd confessed to feeling

Leo's spirit with her, he smiled reassuringly at her, whilst thinking that she was ever so quintessential in the way she was intuitively self-aware and spiritually inclined; especially when she'd supported him through his past issues.

Equally, she had enjoyed hearing about his childhood and teenage years and his loyalty towards his friends when they got into trouble. From what he'd said, she'd gathered that her husband was a creative-minded individual who was willing to take risks.

"Alastair, someone once told me that creative minds are sexy. What's your take on that?"

Without answering, he raised his eyebrows and staring directly at her, he grinned. Almost from the start of their relationship, they'd blended and adapted to each other's mannerisms and subtle gestures.

"I like having you as my muse, Es."

"I'm not your muse, in the sense of the word."

He gave her a sideways glance and her heart flipped. It always did; especially when he looked at her in that seductive way.

The banter continued.

"No, you're not that submissive. Only at those times when you choose to be. To be a muse and a wife is not as difficult as some might imagine."

Amused at his comment, she giggled loudly. His use of the word was meant in an endearing way, albeit said in a jokey manner. There was a lot of truth in it. She was his inspiration. She did instil passion into him, in more ways than one!

Being his muse didn't restrict her own artistic growth. It enhanced it. She was still in control. She still retained her own identity. She was still ambitious and she was still self-disciplined.

"I agree. It's quite an easy role to play and I'm certainly enjoying it."

They understood each other. There was no need for one to dominate the other.

"We're equal. Mutual muses who motivate each other. I wouldn't dare to undermine you, Es. I know your worth. You're such an extremely talented woman and I don't know what I'd do if you weren't in my life."

She quite liked it when he introduced her as his muse and his wife. People would smirk and roll their eyes.

On one occasion, when they were dining out with a newly-acquired friend who was a committed feminist, the fundamental question was raised as to whether the stereotyping of a muse was deemed disrespectful and discriminatory. Remaining silent, Esme had left her friend to form her own opinion.

Noticing that her back was burning, he leant over and began to gently massage some cooling after-sun lotion into her sun-drenched skin.

With senses heightening and anticipation, her erogenous zones tingled as he continued to explore her shapely form.

Within a matter of moments, she was safe in his embrace, enjoying the sensual feel of the ice-cold marble floor beneath her and, with the intensifying heat of her husband's muscular body covering hers, they eagerly demonstrated their love for each other.

fifty

Following a lengthy hike through the scenic terrain not too far from where they lived, they ate lunch in the shade of the overhanging palm tree.

The temperature had already reached 30° and was predicted to reach 35° by mid-afternoon.

Conversation flowed freely, as did the ice-cold Cava.

Already, Esme had noticed yet another side to Alastair's personality. Since spending time alone in Spain, whilst overseeing the completion of the house, he'd become more self-aware.

He'd also noticed a spiritual shift in himself. Letting go of some of his emotional baggage and listening to his inner thoughts had brought about an awakening, which left him with a deep peaceful feeling in his heart.

A pile of books lay on a chair at the side of him.

"They look interesting. What are you reading?"

Noting the cover was tatty and curled at the edges, it was obviously a page-turner.

She smiled when she saw he'd been using a crumpled supermarket receipt for a bookmark. She'd often used them, too.

"It's called The Undiscovered Self. I picked it up the other week at the flea market. I'd been chatting to one of the stallholders and he told me that he'd lived in Manchester before moving to Nerja ten years ago. He claimed that the pace of life and the sun had worked wonders for his physical and mental health. I didn't want to leave without buying anything from him, so I rooted through some cardboard boxes filled with books and then I was drawn to these. I don't know why."

One by one, he passed the books to her. Coelho, Redfield, Chopra, Weiss, Frankl, Ruiz, Dalai Lama and Tolle. All authors she'd read.

Most of her copies were also second-hand buys, having bought them from local library sales and online auctions; although some were new copies.

"Not your usual holiday reads, then?"

Laughing heartily, he winked at her.

She'd first read Jung, as well as other theorists, when she was studying philosophy and psychotherapy.

From reading his first book, his elusiveness had captured her, even though she'd found it difficult to interpret his use of metaphoric. She was a lot younger then.

Throughout her life, she'd read and re-read more of his evocative works, each time discovering more about the man and his perspective on life. Each time, learning something new about herself.

He'd become her 'go to' then and even now, he remained her source of inspiration.

Having been just one of the many authors who'd been instrumental in shaping the way she approached her life, his balanced and enigmatic view of the human psyche and behaviour had interested her the most. He'd left her wondering.

His abstract writing style suited her soul, even though critics of his works, especially fellow scientists, had been frustrated with his revolutionary and complicated views on the interconnectedness of an holistic and synchronistic universe.

"Have you read Jung?"

"Yes. I started reading his books about forty five years ago."

His eyes widened and his jaw dropped.

"I must admit, from what I've read, I found some things in his book rather difficult to understand."

"I did too, at first. It was only later on that I realised that his enigmatic approach was intended to entice the reader into delving into and digesting his theories over a period of time. It's as if he's planting a seed in your mind and then drip-feeding you all the nutrients to enable you to grow into a more self-actualised human being."

"Clever man, then?"

"I would say so. In my estimation, he was an extremely sophisticated philosopher who wrote in a way which gave much meaning to his readers' worlds. Knowing his powerful ethics would generate interest, he was astute enough to realise that those readers would feel the need to dip in and out to learn more about themselves and his beliefs."

Cupping his fist with his chin, he quizzed again.

"Is that what you did?"

She recalled the many synchronicities, signs and communications she'd experienced in her life and how they'd all been linked in one way or another.

"Of course. You can't possibly take it all in at once. From transferring his credible theories into my own way of living, I now completely understand why Jung deliberately pushed his philosophies. It was to encourage a growth mindset where people would become curious enough to explore endless possibilities and be open to further discovering about their own authenticity and the way they behave - and how they fit into the universe."

Hanging onto her every word, he'd just learnt something more about her. A fount of knowledge.

"He also believed that 'education is a kindling of the flame'. He understood that learning by asking was the only way to gain knowledge and to keep on learning by asking more questions to gain wisdom. Much the same as Socrates."

Alastair shivered as the goosebumps rose on his arms. He also was an education enthusiast.

"Another question I'd like to ask you. Tell me about the conscious and the unconscious mind. Explain it to me in a clear way so that I can understand it more."

She was imagining the cogs of his inquisitive brain turning, trying to absorb it all.

"Well, the conscious mind is more concerned with reality, logic and your thoughts and feelings."

"I get that. It's the unconscious mind that I need to know more about."

"Well, it's more personal and unique to you. It holds within it a vast collection of built-up memories from previous lives, as well as some from your present life. Your unconscious influences your conscious. They work together holistically."

As several flashbacks of recent events rushed in, he shuddered. Leaning forward, he wanted more.

"Ok. Carry on."

I will, Socrates! You really are interrogating me."

He grinned and winked at her again.

"We should always pay close attention to our unconscious mind, our intuition. It will never let us down. It may sometimes lead us down a path which we might later think was the wrong one, but it had taken us down that way for a specific reason. Maybe to learn something or as a move towards meeting someone in the future."

Leaving him deep in thought, she went to fetch some iced water. The sweltering sun, coupled with the wine, had left her feeling dehydrated and a little dizzy.

On her return, he was ready to question again.

"I read about collective consciousness. I'm still trying to get my head around it. Sorry if I'm being a pain."

"You're not, darling. It's one of the two layers of our unconscious mind that we already possess when we are reincarnated. One is the personal one, like I said earlier. That part contains occurrences that have been suppressed or forgotten. The collective layer is the deeper of the two and contains a spiritual heritage that has been shared with other humans and species."

Information overload had left his brain buzzing. Swiftly sensing that his processing capacity had been exceeded, she refilled his glass with water and handed it to him.

"Jung believed that all humans are connected to each other through the residues of joint experiences and behaviours with our ancestors."

Nodding in acknowledgement, he grinned.

"Hey, I forgot to tell you something. When I was reading Jung, I discovered that he was involved in the founding of Alcoholics Anonymous. He really did care for his patients, didn't he?

Tilting her head, she smiled. She already knew, but she'd let him have his moment.

"He did."

"Would you say that was a communication or a confirmation, Es?

"What do you think?"

Later, whilst in bed, he was still searching for even more answers. Her inner essence and confident assuredness had captured his curiosity.

She shook her head.

"Haven't you had enough for one day? We'll talk about it again tomorrow."

As she drifted off to sleep, his mind was working overtime, trying to process what he'd recently learnt.

fifty one

"Can we talk about Socrates today, Es?"

The floodgates had opened. He was hungry to learn more.

"Let me see. Where do I start? We've spoken about him briefly before, so you know he was a Greek philosopher who persistently questioned ethics based on human reasoning. He was a humble man really. He loved listening to people and their problems. He saw himself as just an ordinary man, but he was an intelligent non-conformist who was interested in the well-being of society. Like Jung, he also believed that the universe is innately connected and that we all have an obligation to care for our fellow humans. His motto was to be kind, because everyone we meet is fighting their own battles."

Alastair reflected on how he'd connected with Ali and how that first fortuitous meeting had been instrumental in bringing about a change in his own life. Through his volunteering roles and his new job Ali was now being 'of-service' to others. His life had also changed.

"Socrates had witnessed extreme poverty and homelessness around him each day and, though he knew he couldn't personally eradicate it, he donated some of his money to the poor, declaring that he still had enough to live a comfortable lifestyle."

Immediately, he thought of Mr Hoffman and his decision to renovate the rest of the building for other homeless projects, even saying he wanted to eventually sign it over to the charity. He'd also said the same thing about having more than enough to live on and that the building would be put to better use than being left empty.

"Something's happening here, Es. When you said about us all being innately connected, in my mind's eye I'm seeing so many synchronicities with where we are at this moment in time. It's seeming like you're playing a word association game with me. I'm relating everything you've said over the last few days to many people who are in our current circle. Why are all these things happening now?"

It was discernible that an additional spiritual awakening was taking place. As she'd been talking, she'd felt as if there was someone standing over her, putting words in her mouth. It wouldn't be the first time and she knew it wouldn't be the last.

Throwing it back at him, it was her turn to ask the question.

"Why do *you* think it's happening, Alastair?"

Placing the palm of his hand over his mouth, he didn't answer straight away. Patiently, she waited.

"Synchronicity? A significant sign from the universe? A series of intertwined events which brings unknown people together, for the purpose of helping each other?"

"Yes. All of those. On the day you met Ali, you began inviting meaningful coincidences into your life. He was the one who released something in you that has always been there; but more so since your dad's tragic experiences."

Tilting his head slightly, he nodded.

"Maybe that was the precise moment, that your unconscious and your collective unconscious,

232

mutually decided the purpose of your personal mission would be to make a positive impact on the lives of the homeless. Ali had clearly brought the obvious to the forefront. Through him, you then met Ollie and the unfortunate incident occurred, which then forced you to re-evaluate what you wanted out of life. Whatever you saw in him, had evoked compassion for his cause and motivated you not to judge him and turn away from his suffering".

Her meaningful words resonated and a sudden warm feeling entered his heart.

"You're right, Es. You're right."

"No doubt that there'll have been many other signs over the years that have been unfolding, but you hadn't been paying much attention to them. The time wouldn't have been right then, anyhow. It was the right time when you encountered him. He helped to remind you of the person you really are."

"Do you think me being drawn to those books was another sign? Do you think I'm being guided by someone or something so that I can see what needs to be done?"

"It's up to you to determine the meaning of the communications. You need to discover your own answers. Try to be patient when reading the books. If you persist, something will click and the words will then become much clearer to you. Socrates was a great believer of educating the self, through reading or through life experiences and he believed that virtue is knowledge and can't be taught. Patience is a virtue, Alastair. It's good for our souls, so be patient."

He laughed at her subtle humour.

Trying to keep a straight face, she turned her head slightly.

"Are you laughing at me, Mr Brickman?"

"Would I? I'm admiring your layers of earthly wisdom. I didn't know that you knew so much. When I question you, I'm not doubting you. I just want to find answers and you do explain it better."

Grinning, she teased him again.

"Not doubting. I should hope not! Just being inquisitive."

Far from being fazed by his incessant requests for information, she'd liked regurgitating and relaying what she'd learnt over the years.

Socrates' words rang in her ears. – 'Education is a kindling of the flame'. She was enjoying kindling her husband's flame. From her own experiences, she knew that continual questioning and the gathering of information was the only way to gain knowledge; whether it be trivial or important learning, through conversation or listening, reading or just observing others. It had helped in her endeavour to become a better human being.

Over the past few days, she'd contemplated on those mutual connections between what they'd discussed and those transpiring synchronicities; or communications as she preferred to call them.

Like Jung and Socrates, her and Alastair were non-conformists to a degree. As a young child and whilst growing up, she'd continually challenged and pestered her parents, teachers and friends until she got the answer she wanted – the 'truth'. Alastair, especially when applying his own creativity to the extreme, had always challenged boundaries and opened people's minds to taking risks with new ideas.

Recently, she'd had more than a glimpse into the window of her husband's mind. Socrates believed in justice and he had faith in mankind. So did her husband, especially when he believed that Ollie had the desire to reinvent himself and he hadn't wanted to press charges against him.

Similarly, Alastair acquired a glut of unfamiliar knowledge and had learnt more about her.

"Would you say I was a work in progress, Es?"

"We all are."

With the amount of dialogue and introspection which had taken place recently, it would appear that the Jungian disciple and the loyal follower of Socrates were well matched!

fifty two

It was early December when they arrived in England on the late evening flight.

The expected, yet unwelcome bitter cold and wet weather greeted them as they descended the plane steps. Wishing they'd worn warmer clothes, they hurried along the walkways into the terminal building.

Halfway into the journey back to Manchester, both had constantly sneezed. Most of the passengers were doing the same. Some were multi-sneezing and others just seemed to follow on in relay.

Before moving through the passport control, Alastair had texted Stefano to say they'd landed.

He was already waiting in the car park and had them home in no time.

Fortunately, a warm house awaited them as they opened the entrance door. The intelligent house system had seen to that.

"Shall we have a drink, Es?"

"Yes, please. A peppermint tea for me."

"I'm having a brandy. I can't get warm."

Despite the heating flowing throughout the house, she started to shiver and hugged herself.

"Great idea. I'll have one too, as well as the peppermint. I'm thirsty. My throat's a bit sore. I think it must have been the air conditioning on the plane."

She was undressed and in bed, tucked under the duvet, still shivering, before he brought the drinks to her.

"I can't get warm either, Alastair."

Placing them on the side table, he took a blanket out of a storage unit and wrapped it around her shoulders.

"Have this brandy. It'll warm you up."

Slowly sipping the clear amber liquid, she held it on her tongue before swallowing it. The warm sensation immediately touched her stomach and she emptied the glass.

He'd quickly downed his drink in one go.

His teeth were chattering as he slid into bed at the side of her.

Although the brandy had immediately taken effect, their slumber had been far from sound, or soundless. Each coughed in tandem, as they tossed and turned trying to get comfortable as sleep evaded them.

He looked at his watch again. 5.45am.

"Do you want a drink, Es?"

"I'd love one. Just hot water for me, please. I feel as if I'm coming down with a heavy cold. I hope it's not flu."

"Me too. I feel dreadful. If it is, I bet we've caught it from Miguel and Sofia when we were out walking with them. They'd been in bed for a week, full of it, before we came home."

"Could you see if we have any flu capsules and bring a couple of dry biscuits too. I don't want to take medication on an empty stomach."

"I think I'll need some, too."

They awoke at noon. The medication had done its job, but they still felt rough and still felt cold.

Snuggling into each other to keep warm, they listened to the comforting sound of heavy pelting rain, accompanied by sudden gusts of wind pouring down

237

the full-length panes.

"Do you know, Es. We've not been feeling 100% for the last week, have we? We weren't as active as we usually are."

"No. We've both been lethargic. You didn't even feel like going for your morning run."

An unexpected flash of lighting flew past and startled them.

"No. It's not like me to miss my exercise. You know what I'm like. I need to run. How are you feeling now?"

"I feel nauseous and my stomach's griping. I think I may need to eat. We haven't eaten, except for a few biscuits since we left Spain yesterday evening, but the thought of food turns my stomach."

He started to cough again and his ribs felt sore.

"A little porridge might settle our stomachs. I'll make some."

For the remainder of the day, they stayed in bed, in and out of sleep, feeling worse as evening fell.

"Do we have any more medication, Alastair?"

Sitting up, she quickly grabbed a tissue from the side table and sneezed into it. Multiple sneezes later and she felt weaker than before.

"It's more than a cold, isn't it? It's got to be flu."

Passing her a glass of water and two capsules, she swallowed it quickly and lay back down. He took the same and waited for them to kick in.

"It's got to be."

They drifted off again, only to be woken four hours later by Alastair's chesty cough, which made his eyes water and seemed to last for up to a minute.

"Sit up, darling. It might ease it."

238

He didn't have the energy to lift himself up. His muscles hurt and he had a burning sensation at the back of his throat.

"I can't. I feel awful."

She got out of bed and handed him a glass of water, before placing an extra pillow behind his neck.

Shifting his body, he manoeuvred himself into an upright position, but was still uncomfortable. It felt as if there was a heavy weight pressing down on his chest.

"Is that any better?"

Thankful for all her endeavours, he nodded. He didn't want her to fret. She was ill too.

"A little, thanks."

Aware that his sickness was worsening and, trying not to show her fears, she pulled the quilt up over his shoulders.

"Are there any flu capsules left?"

"I think we have enough to see us through till morning."

Going downstairs, she nearly tripped and only just managed to save herself and the glass carafe she had in her hand. If only she'd switched on the light!

Feeling woozy, she filled the carafe with water, collected the packet of biscuits and returned to the bedroom.

Climbing the stairs had stripped her energy. Her legs ached, her arms felt weak and her eyeballs ached.

Huddled together, they lay there, listening to the relentless pelting of the rain, waiting for sleep to come.

fifty three

Over the following six days, things got worse before they got better.

Alastair's condition deteriorated. His hot and cold episodes saw times when he'd throw the duvet off, only to quickly drag it back a few minutes later when he started shivering.

The prolonged night sweats were the worst. At one point, his temperature reached 38° and he felt as if he was on fire. He resorted to sleeping naked and, because he was endlessly moving around the bed to find a cold spot, Esme moved into one of the guest rooms.

Whilst both displayed similar symptoms, there were some differences. Her husband's indicators were more severe.

He'd never experienced any feelings like them before or, felt as ill. Exhausted, his body cried out for sleep, but even after taking paracetamol, he could still feel pain in his muscles and bones.

Walking a short distance to the en-suite had wiped him out. His legs felt too heavy to carry his body.

It was when he suddenly became breathless that Esme panicked.

Flashbacks of the time when the paramedics had last been in the house beside his bed, added to her already-perplexed state of mind.

She'd immediately rang the GP's surgery and, after relaying all of his symptoms, was given a swift diagnosis of a bad dose of flu with the advice to keep taking the medication and drinking plenty of fluids..

Her matter of urgency, although not wholly dismissed, hadn't been viewed as being critical enough to require a home visit, even though she thought it was!

Whilst rushing downstairs to get some ice to make a cold compress, she'd nearly tripped again.

She'd lain, by his side, sharing her last bit of energy with him until he'd finally drifted off, before finally allowing herself some much-needed sleep.

Her own physical and mental strength had waned rapidly and disorientation, combined with severe fatigue, had all but wiped her out. She hadn't known what day it was, or what time it was, or what she was meant to be doing. Her befuddled brain couldn't cope.

The room had stank of illness and sweat and having had little strength, she'd struggled to open the sliding door leading out onto the balcony to let some fresh air in.

Frustrated, she'd cried again.

Her simmering headache had developed into an unbearable one and it had suddenly dawned on her that she was probably dehydrated and, so was Alastair.

Following several phone calls to see if they were okay, Camellia had kindly been leaving fresh batches of consommé and chicken soup on their doorstep each day, which they had managed to swallow, although they'd not been able to taste it. They'd eaten a few biscuits and drank a little water with their medication, but during all of the mayhem, she'd forgotten to replenish the carafe with water; hence her confused state, light-headedness and muscle cramps.

By the end of the sixth day, after managing to catch up on her sleep, she'd felt better. Alastair had also shown signs of recovery, which eased her mind.

She'd returned to the marital bed to sleep at his side. She'd needed a hug and she'd needed to feel the warmth of his body against hers.

Within the space of six days, their appearances had changed. His facial hair had grown, revealing a salt and pepper beard and his weight loss was visible, as was Esme's. On looking closely in the mirror, a pale gaunt face stared back at her.

She'd been surprised that he'd been affected more than her by the flu. He'd always been physically fitter than her and she'd thought he was the stronger.

His stubborn cough had lingered and, on several occasions, he had thought the flu might be returning, when he'd woken up with a throbbing headache and a buzzing in his ears.

Mindful of getting sufficient rest, their energy had returned slowly, thanks to the kindness of Stefano and Camellia who'd delivered freshly cooked food from their restaurant each day.

It had been a tough week, but they'd survived it!

Without respecting her own need for rest, she had made her husband's health her priority. Although fragile, her resilience had been stronger than his and she'd taken control. It was a necessity.

Her resilience and devoted resolve had been the same when she'd lovingly nursed Leo during his final days.

Pushed beyond what she thought were her utmost limits, she'd stayed hopeful.

242

The fog had lifted.

Neither had experienced anything like it before and they hoped that they'd never experience anything like it again!

fifty four

During the week leading up to Christmas, Alastair and Esme had ordered online gifts for their neighbours and Ali. They'd also sent toiletry hampers to the Habitaire residents and luxury food hampers to the staff and support workers.

A pleasant Christmas Eve had been spent at the chantry ruins with their neighbours, singing carols, drinking mulled wine and eating mince pies. Lights had been erected around the ruins and they'd all huddled together around a large outdoor heater, with thick fluffy blankets to keep warm.

After spending their first Christmas Day as a married couple on their own, cooking together and watching television, they'd felt well enough to accept an invite to a Boxing Day dinner from Stefano and Camellia.

The following days had mainly consisted of impromptu naps, gentle walks along the country lane at the rear of their house and meaningful discussions.

On New Year' Eve, they had accepted yet another invite to an informal evening where Stefano had served a traditional Lancashire hotpot with red cabbage and chunks of crusty bread.

During regular telephone conversations with Mateo, Alastair had discovered that 'someone in the know' had heard rumours that Spanish virologists had found traces of a coronavirus in some samples of wastewater which had been collected in March 2019.

Whilst keeping a close eye on the news, it had

been revealed that two UK residents who had been working in Wuhan had tested positive for Coronavirus after arriving in England on 29th January 2020. More passengers who were also on the plane had to spend fourteen days in quarantine in Merseyside.

On February 1st, Mateo had telephoned again to say that Spain had confirmed its first case of Coronavirus in the Canary Islands.

Although they'd previously booked flights to return to their home in Spain, they decided against it. It was too risky. Mateo would check in on their property whilst they were away.

fifty five

Alastair's interest in philosophy and the psyche hadn't waned. When his head wasn't buried in a book, he was busy gathering more information from the internet. At times, he'd take himself off to the chantry to sit quietly on the bench.

Following their recent bout of flu, Esme had also been recuperating by resting and re-reading some of her books and design magazines. Whilst her mind was more alert now, fatigue still lingered.

Armed with two mugs of hot chocolate, a writing pad and pen, he spied his chance and joined her on the sofa.

She'd been expecting her sleuth of a husband to instigate another investigative conversation. A change in his behaviour and his heightened curiosity in developing his intuition, were just a few of the signs.

"Do you know that it's only just over a year since we first met?"

She nodded. Recollecting the first time they'd spoken on the phone, she intuitively knew that she'd be with him.

In discovering more about themselves, they'd become more spiritually and physically intimate; both displaying an increased attentiveness to each other's needs.

Self-disclosures had become commonplace in their day to day lives. Esme would often recall her times with Leo and her love for him. Alastair would also slip in some relevant faux pas into their lengthy conversations. With personal values aligned, their shared emotional and insightful snippets had further enhanced their well-being.

"I wonder what led me to you, Es."

Resting the palm of her hand on her chin, she raised her left eyebrow and pursed her lips.

"Some would say that like attracts like. Others might say we share a past life connection and during our pre-birth planning, we'd agreed to meet again to resolve unfinished business."

He knew that would be one of her answers.

"This last year feels like it's been an unfolding mystery of sorts. I can't explain it. I'm trying to grasp the continuous string of events that led us to where we are now."

Resting her hand on his knee, she gazed into his eyes as he asked another question.

"Can I ask you something? Would you happen to be an old soul? It's just that I've been reading about them and you seem to know a lot of things at a deeper level."

"We both are, Alastair. We came into this life with an agenda to grow together and to reach others. There was an instant spiritual connection for me when I first heard your voice. It just took you a little longer to recognise the link. I feel it happened for you when you came back after seeing Jen. Anyhow you, less of the old!"

He grinned. Slowly processing what she'd said, he leant back and closed his eyes.

"I've been thinking about Socrates when he said that happiness isn't found in material things and that human relationships are far more important. He meant it was about recognising what we already have and not what we don't have, or what we want to have, didn't he?"

"I suppose his message was that, if we're not contented with ourselves, then we will never be contented with what we'd like to have. He says that being content means you're thankful for all what you have, without seeking fulfilment in obtaining more possessions. He also believed that if we're contented, we're naturally healthy and he deemed that excess luxury was artificial poverty."

Esme pondered on how her husband had been doing a lot of thinking lately!

fifty six

Esme had spent several days, sorting through her vast collection of designer clothes and accessories. Having no great need for them anymore, she'd decided to place them in the hands of an auctioneer who'd hold a private event for those famous local celebrities who'd be willing to splash their cash.

Wanting to remain anonymous, she wouldn't be present. Her life was so different now. She'd kept some of the dresses that Leo had bought for her, so that when she did wear them, they'd be a reminder of the precious times with him .

In recognising the change of priorities in her own life, she thought of how the celebrities she'd occasionally mixed with, were both vulnerable and brave at the same time. By opening their lives to the world, it was an expectation that there'd be some criticism of their lifestyles. However, several times, they'd admitted that they'd found it difficult to deal with negative attacks about their fame, wealth and extravagant behaviours. They'd also confessed that, in order to retain their desired celebrity status, they had no choice other than to continue oversharing every positive and negative aspect of their personal lives. It was a vital necessity, to not only feed their own insecurities, but more importantly to keep the extortionate amount of money rolling in.

A staggering total of almost £100,000 had been acquired from the auction of her once-prized possessions. The proceeds had been equally divided between Habitaire and several homeless charities.

Following the disclosure on 10th March 2020, that a government minister had tested positive for coronavirus, it had dawned on her and Alastair that their symptoms had been exactly the same as those that had been disclosed on the news channels.

At the time of their illness, it had been mooted that they'd contracted a flu virus. They'd recalled how there'd been a one-week incubation period, where they'd felt weak. A week of debilitating symptoms had quickly materialised and, whilst it had taken another week to recover, intermittent periods of fatigue had remained with them.

On reflection, although the virus they'd had was not officially confirmed, they'd felt certain that they'd been infected with the Coronavirus. Their healthy lifestyle hadn't even protected them from contracting it!

fifty seven

On the afternoon of the Celebration of Achievement Event, the attendees all congregated in the spacious hallway.

Initially, he hadn't recognised Ollie. It was only when he'd heard his voice, that he turned around.

There was a discernible difference in the way he looked now, to when he'd seen him yesterday. Without facial hair and a shaggy long hairstyle, he was unrecognisable and yet, the more Alastair looked at him, the more he felt that there was something oddly familiar about him.

"I didn't recognise you then."

"Thought I'd betta look presentable for the occasion."

Although they were polite with each other and Alastair had forgiven him, there was still an underlying uncomfortableness which hadn't fully been dealt with.

"Ollie, this is my wife, Esme."

He knew this moment would come and he'd been dreading it. Shifting from side to side, he took a step back, his internalised mortification expressing itself in his reddened face.

She hadn't known how she'd react when she eventually came face to face with him. Being aware of having preconceptions, she'd promised herself that she would assess the situation objectively and without any prejudice.

"Hello. Pleased to meet you."

Stuttering his reply, he hung his head.

"Hello Mrs Brickman. Pleased to meet yer too."

"Are you ready for this, Ollie?"

Shrugging his shoulders, he grimaced.

"Think so."

He was so glad they hadn't offered to shake his hand. His palm was sweaty and he was trembling.

As part of his rehabilitation programme, he'd already completed some emotional purging; opening several excruciating wounds in his arduous effort to move forward. He knew it wouldn't be an instant fix. It was a work in progress. There was still a lot of hurt buried within him.

After seeking professional advice and being given permission from Ollie's psychotherapist, Alastair had encouraged him to bring his narrative to life at the event.

"He's not anything like I expected him to be", she whispered.

A cloak of disbelief, coupled with compassion, enfolded her. His sad blue eyes revealed the haunted look of a lost soul and his bent posture revealed signs of stress and inner sadness.

As the event commenced, the sounds of 'Bridge Over Troubled Water' resounded throughout the building and as Alastair caught Ali's eye, they both lowered their heads once in acknowledgement. He was four months into his new job and loving it.

Esme tapped into the energy in the room and, observing the behaviour of certain individuals, her social instincts quickly deduced that Ollie had become an admired leader of the group.

One young man, whose skin appeared grey and wrinkled, stood near him and followed his every move. Esme had gained first-hand experience of this type of worship/attachment syndrome when she had worked at the women's refuge.

Whilst Ollie prepared himself, Alastair opened the celebration, thanking his colleagues, neighbours and everyone who'd been involved in bringing the project to fruition. Whereas he'd been the driving force behind it, none of it would have happened without the people who'd shared and contributed to his vision. Their selfless acts were already having a reverberating effect on the men who currently lived here and on those who had left, having found employment and other accommodation.

Esme couldn't help thinking of how her first and second husbands were similar, in terms of their belief that sharing and caring was important. Both had shown and stretched their compassion, by helping those who were suffering and in need.

With tension escalating, Ollie stood before his audience, clearing his throat numerous times. Eyes, blinking rapidly, he leant on the lectern and gripped it before reading from his notes.

"Hello everyone. On behalf of all of us 'ere, I wannna welcome youse and thank all of youse who've supported us and walked amongst us."

Understandably so, his voice was wobbly. He stopped to take a few deep breaths and viewed his spectators.

"We've asked arselves many times, how we gorrin to the state we were in and we all 'ave our own 'orror stories to tell. Our lived experiences 'ave 'elped us to 'elp each other. We know, only too well, how some people looked down on us when we were out there on the streets."

Unable to disguise his unnerving fear of speaking in front of an audience, his knees started to shake and, as he strived to regain his composure, his trusty devotee moved in closer.

His jaw tightened. Lifting his thumb to his mouth, he blew on it ten times, before bravely continuing.

"We've learned to accept the stigmatisation and discrimination, although it has been ard, like. It's a given that the majority of people will see us as being lesser than them. Even some of our own families 'ave rejected us."

Esme had recently devoured a document, which stated exactly what Ollie was saying. Data had revealed that a sizeable proportion of society, neither accept or choose to understand the human rights of the vulnerable population and their sombre homeless predicament.

"We're all working 'ard, with the 'elp of youse guys, to stay away from the booze and the drugs. We're glad to be away from Cardboard City, but we do 'ave feelings of survival guilt for our mates who are still out there freezin and for them who've died on the streets."

Again, he had to stop. Pursing his lips and taking several deep breaths, he straightened his back.

"We're all tackling our addictions in the best ways we can. Facing our fears, bit by bit. There's always a voice naggin us, tempting us. We're trying to reinvent ourselves and break the cycle, as our support workers would say. 'Aving some lessons 'ere in the Learnin Room and spending most of our days in therapy units, has really 'elped us. We've been doin some creative writing and some maths and some music therapy. It's been great for our mental health and managing our feelings. We all talk about our own problems and we've even passed some Functional Skills exams. All of us 'ave got support plans and we're sticking to 'em. We know we 'ave to stick to the rules, or else we're outta this place."

The other guys behind him were nodding. Some were continuing their studies within Further Education colleges and two of the previous residents had gained apprenticeships with local businesses.

"Some people out there can't see our worth, but that doesn't mean we're worthless. We've all 'ad to work on improving our self-worth. It's been tough, but we're getting there. We're not goin back. We're only movin forward. Trying to get back our identity."

"No, mate. We're definitely not goin that way", a voice piped up from beside him.

Esme thought once more about Nunchi and its absence in society; reflecting on the misinterpretation and misunderstanding of homelessness and the many difficulties people faced due to a lack of compassion, consideration and acceptance.

Sensing that some of the audience, as well as the men themselves, may have perceived failure to have taken place, she only saw completed growth of the soul in these courageous men who were stood before her.

"We're so grateful that we live 'ere. We feel safe and all we know how fortunate we are. Very fortunate! We never imagined we could live in a place like this. When we first came 'ere, it was beyond our expectations. Youse can see how tidy we keep it. We're very proud of it. It's great to 'ave some private space and our own door keys."

One of men behind him interjected.

"Don't forget to tell 'em about how we've gorra a rota to do the jobs in 'ere and some of us 'ave got part-time jobs. Go on, mate. Tell 'em."

"Alright, lad. I think you already 'ave."

Laughter erupted as he waited for quiet before continuing.

"So, we just want ya to know that we all feel positive about our futures. It's not gonna to be easy for us, but we're gerrin there. Shakespeare once said that we 'old our destiny in ourselves, so all of us in 'ere are doin the best we can to take back control of our lives."

All having their own challenges, the other men nodded and his sidekick agreed with him.

"Yeah, we are. Yeah, yeah, yeah. Dead right we are, mate. We're gonna do it, aren't we mate? We've come a long way, haven't we mate? We'll only fail if we quit and we're not quitting, are we?"

A voice piped in from the back of the room.

"The only thing is, that some of the other guys on the streets, now think that we're better than 'em and we're not, are we?"

He looked around and the men were shaking their heads. It was as if Ollie was the protagonist on a theatre stage and the others had supporting roles in the play. It was evident that his vibration of hope had spread through to the others.

His life challenges and the way in which he'd broken through his years of suffering, had given growth to his soul and spirit. He was now curious to embrace other life lessons in more joyful ways. Spending more time with his precious daughter was just one of those ways. Helping others to heal was

256

another.

During some of the rehabilitation sessions, they'd all shared their own personal experiences of being undervalued, humiliated and ignored, but they were now growing stronger and moving forward with their lives.

"Some of our mates on the streets don't wanna know us now, or even lerrus help 'em."

Ollie allowed a few moments to pass.

"Anyhow, before I finish, I just wanna thank all youse guys, the support services team and the chaplain again. During our weekly chats, he's really made us feel included. He said that in the eyes of God, we're all his children and we shouldn't forget it. For most of me life, I've doubted meself many times. I've faced need and loss in me life, but I've found me spark again and I'm startin to believe in meself. I'm startin to love meself. I've hated meself for so long, but I'm startin to trust meself and I can see things differently now. I know there's a greater meanin behind what I've been through."

His mates nodded, all shouting "Yeah, Yeah!"

"Sorry for goin on, but can I just tell yer that when I was goin through all that dead-bad stuff, somethin made me wanna drag meself out of it. Call it God. Call it being saved. Call it what you wanna call it. I don't know worrit was. All I know is that I'm 'ere now and I'm doin ok. I have 'ope."

As he raised his hands to his eyes, his devotee placed an arm around his back and leant into him.

Esme smiled as she remembered when God's name had also featured in the opening event.

"Aw, mate! Come on mate. You'll be ok."

Composing himself once more, he cleared his

throat and resumed his lengthy monologue.

"Sorry again. Just one last thing and then I'll shurrup. Promise ya. Since I came 'ere, I've been gerrin back into readin books and writin again. I know now that I'm me own keeper and I've got the power to change me life and that's what I'm doin. I've worked on lerrin go of the 'what if's'. I've written a poem, which I'd like yer all to listen to, so that ya know, youse can really understand what we're goin through and see it from our point of view. I written a few more and me social worker thinks I should write a book. Ha-ha!"

Intentionally stopping for a few moments as he'd been advised to do, to give the audience time to reflect, he feigned forgetfulness as he looked down at his notes.

Esme had been touched by his speech. The men weren't worthless at all. Their shared openness was both humbling and healing. It was crucial to their recovery and to raising awareness of the human suffering which was being ignored. She saw great power in their open honesty. The homeless should be supported more and understood, rather than them being shunned and reprimanded for living on the streets.

Their visibility was such a glaring reminder for society to be less judgemental. Instead of ostracising and segregating vulnerable people, she truly hoped that society would find some compassion to recognise the devastating impact that homelessness has on society. Her wish was that cohesive measures would be adopted, instead of isolating susceptible people.

Fully aware that individuals can only follow their own pathway in life, she was also mindful that several of these individuals could have deliberately

258

chosen to reincarnate, as so to experience numerous intensive events; episodes which would develop their souls and benefit them in understanding how precious human life is. In living out their lives in a particular way, experiencing the pain and rejection that social stigma brings, she felt certain that they were balancing their own karma and helping others to balance theirs, too.

From a soul perspective, she also believed what Ollie and the other men had been through, was not a mistake. The universe had responded with several 'dark' events to force change in their lives and by experiencing powerlessness, it had given them the power to move forward; thereby furthering their spiritual growth.

She also considered that their suffering could be a mechanism for forcing a crucial shift in human evolvement.

Scanning the room again, she thought how every person within this collective space was meant to be here in this moment in time; for whatever reason that may be! As the avid listeners silently absorbed Ollie's truthfulness, she could hear several men sniffing and sensed that his own awakening had helped to awaken their feelings.

His vulnerability had empowered him with the courage to stand up in front of an audience and bare his soul. Ollie's story, although not entirely unique, had demanded to be heard! Just before he was about to read his poem, he plucked up the courage to share his shame resilience, once more.

"Sorry again. I know I failed meself and others, many times. I had to keep tryin' and lookin for a meanin' to me life. I was selfish. I chose alcohol and drugs over 'er 'appiness, but finally I saw the light. The memory of when I first held 'er little body in me arms, 'elped me to concentrate on me recovery."

A convulsive gasp escaped from his throat and he bowed his head quickly in embarrassment.

"The real meanin to me life is me daughter. She needs 'er arl dad and that's why I can't go back to that dark place. She needs me and I need 'er! I really do!"

Esme inhaled. His suffering had obviously been instrumental in shaping his life in ways that he'd never thought was possible. It'd been a process of identifying what he really wanted from his life. Seeing beyond the physical, she was so aware that society and, most of those present, would not yet understand what he might have gained and might still be gaining from his glut of extreme adversities.

Standing upright, he took a few deep breaths and introduced his poem. "It's called, They Don't fit Me.

Try me shoes on
For just one day
They weigh a ton
I'm sure you'd say

They don't fit me
No doubt, you'd plead
No, you cannot see
How me mind, it doth bleed

Try 'em on
I say again
These shoes I don
Are filled with pain

No comments vent
On what you see
My mind is pent
Whilst yours is free

They won't fit you
You say, too tight
Wrong size, you rue
Of that you're re right!

A rousing applause echoed loudly throughout the space, with enthusiastic shouts of, 'Well done, mate'.

His intelligent and profound message had been crystal clear. No one *would* want to be in his shoes! He'd endured a burdensome chapter and was in the process of transitioning from dependency to a dry, clean lifestyle.

His carefully chosen words had hit the mark and she felt sure that much healing had taken place within the room. Much value had been gained from exposing his vulnerabilities.

Following a short interval, Alastair and Esme presented certificates to the men.

He shook Ollie's hand.

"I know I've sed this many times, but I'm truly sorry and ashamed for worra did to yer. Hey, did yer know that yer name means defender of mankind?"

"Like I've said before, I've already forgiven

261

you. No, I didn't know that."

Collecting his certificate from Esme, he walked back to join the rest of the group. He knew he'd so much to be grateful for. Whilst in rehabilitation, he'd utilised his time to assess his own inability to learn from his addictions and repeated hurting - and more so, the hurt he'd caused others. He hadn't realised that one day, his weaknesses and his deepest fears would become his strengths. By crossing that bridge, he'd gained faith in his ability to move on.

In endeavouring to understand his attacker's predicament, Alastair had unknowingly assisted Ollie in manifesting his own resolve to get help.

Once all the certificates had been distributed, everyone congregated in the lounge and the kitchen area for refreshments. Some guests were shown inside the Learning Room, where the men's writings and artwork adorned the walls.

Alastair and Esme had remained in the lounge area, watching the residents as they all eagerly engaged in lively conversation. The kitchen area had brought back unwanted memories for him and, as he leant with his back against the wall, he felt protected; safe in the knowledge that no one could approach him from behind.

On occasions, his conscience pricked him, for having what he had; his skills, his wealth, his comforts and his driving ambition to succeed. Yes, he'd worked hard for all of it. Opportunities had come his way and he'd grabbed them with both hands, but he still felt some concern for those individuals who'd experienced and were still experiencing, what his own father had gone through whilst being homeless.

He thought of Frank Lloyd Wright's meaningful

words, knowing that he, Esme and his friends had given 'reason, rhyme and meaning' to the lives of the people who were living here.

"I heard what he said to you, Alastair. You **are** a defender of mankind."

Not knowing how to respond, he nudged her.

"What does your name mean, Es?"

"It means love."

Placing his arm around her waist, he held his precious muse close and gently kissed the nape of her neck.

"Well, that is very apt."

After bidding their farewells, they'd only just stepped out onto the bustling street, when Ollie approached them.

"Mr Brickman. I just wanna thank yer again for what yer did for me. Whilst I've been living 'ere, I've been doin some research into me family tree. Both of me parents are dead now, but I've discovered somethin interestin."

"Oh! I'm so sorry to hear about your parents, but I'm glad you've found some details about them."

Overpowered with mounting trepidation, Ollie hesitated; his eyes misty, his body quivering and his voice hoarse. He was so remorseful for what he'd done. His heart was still heavy.

"Alastair, I'm yer half-brother."

*"The mission of an architect is
to help people understand
how to make life more beautiful,
the world a better one for living in and
to give reason, rhyme and meaning to life"*

Frank Lloyd Wright 1957

epilogue

Whilst his father had been working away for long periods of time, his mother had known that her husband was seeing other women. Alastair also had an inkling. When he was a teenager, his father had introduced his many lady friends to him on several occasions, always stressing that they were colleagues.

What he didn't know, was that his mother had started a love affair with one of her neighbours and had become pregnant.

On a very rare occasion, when his father had returned home, she was already three months pregnant. Having always worn loose clothes, as she'd carried some weight, her pregnancy wasn't that noticeable.

When her baby was due, it was the school summer holidays and she'd sent twelve-year-old Alastair and his older brother to stay with her sister for two weeks.

After her son was born, she was allowed to keep him with her for a week, before handing him over to foster parents. The boy was given the name, Oliver Anderson. Her maiden name had been Mary Olivia Anderson.

Whilst police investigations were being undertaken, Alastair had been informed that his attacker's name was Oliver Anderson. He'd been slightly startled by the familiar resemblance to his mother's maiden name, but he'd been in too much shock to think more about it.

Olivia had continued seeing her lover, even when her husband found out. It had sent him off the rails and that was when his business went bust, along with his sanity.

It had been ok for him to have affairs and yet, he was furious when he found out his wife was doing the same. He'd begged her to end the affair and, when she refused, he gone around to where the man lived and battered him.

Ollie's foster parents, who later became his adoptive parents, didn't change his surname.

His childhood hadn't been a good one. He'd been sorely ridiculed for having a different name to his parents. Having gotten in with the wrong crowd, he didn't have a chance.

When he'd first met the mother of his child, she was also substance and alcohol dependent. After their baby girl was born, she was diagnosed with Neonatal Abstinence Syndrome and had been very poorly.

Sadly, soon after giving birth, his partner had died of a massive overdose.

Like her father had been, the baby was also fostered.

After developing several neurodevelopmental traits, she'd been diagnosed with autism and other health issues.

On the occasions when Alastair had seen him with his daughter, the court had granted him an hour's access a week. At that time, he'd desperately wanted to care for his daughter. Whilst his heart ached for her, his desire for his dependencies had been far stronger. Try as he might, he couldn't exist without them.

At those access times, Ollie hadn't realised

that her foster parents had been covertly following them, ready to seize her if things got out of hand.

After having several challenging relapses, Ollie had remained dry and clean for a lengthy period of time. In his heart, he knew that he had to do it for his daughter. The courts had allowed him extra access and they were slowly rebuilding a family relationship.

Alastair's mother and Ollie's father had taken their secret with them to their graves.

Ollie had often wondered why his parents hadn't tried to locate him. He didn't even have a photograph of them.

Alastair also found it hard to understand how a mother could leave her son.

Neither of them would know, now!

How could they both, ever be expected, to understand how tremendously torturous it must have been for her to hand over her newborn son, knowing that she'd probably never see him again?

reflection

Considering the norms of what society deems to be the correct way to behave and the constant pressures of how one should be living their life, is it appropriate that one disapproving human should impose and coerce their will on another?

Is attempting to interfere with and live someone else's unique life journey ever acceptable?

More significantly, should we not acknowledge that life is not solely about the 'have' and the 'have-nots'?

Whether wealthy or poor, shouldn't we try to accept that all humans tread their own path, make their own individual choices, deal with their own struggles and harrowing ordeals, in their own inimitable ways?

Do those who have been upwardly mobile, both socially and economically, deserve criticism for striving to achieve and following their own authentic route?

In questioning whether someone is deserving or undeserving, entitled or not entitled, is it fitting that one human feels it is acceptable to make a judgement about whether his fellow humans are worthy or unworthy?

Is it realistic to imagine that, sometime in the future, society will be able to overcome all differences and inequalities?

Considering human evolution requires change, is it then reasonable to consider the possibility that we are all spiritual catalysts in one way or another;

271

magnetically drawn to certain individuals, with the foremost aim of transforming one another's lives?

about the author

Susan Higgins is a semi-retired educator of English, a fictional/technical author and an accomplished facilitator of change.

As an author of fiction, her previous works have been inspired by the picturesque Languedoc region of France, her perpetual passion for her own self-development and the advancement of others, on both an academic level and a spiritual level.

As a non-fictional author, her writings have included technical operating procedures and multiple media periodicals for several reputable organisations.

Over the past two decades, with the main purpose of supporting and developing those with learning differences and mental health issues, she has resourcefully designed, implemented and delivered countless creative writing sessions, educational programmes and self-development courses.

Her role as a personal tutor to children who have various learning differences and disabilities, continues to be a significant part of her existence.

Thank you for choosing my book.
If you've enjoyed reading it,
I'd be most grateful if
you'd leave a review
on amazon.co.uk

Printed in Great Britain
by Amazon

16481778R00158